DASHING THROUGH THE FEAR

A SLEIGHVILLE NOVEL
BOOK 1

AMANDA SIEGRIST

ALSO BY AMANDA SIEGRIST

A happy ending is all I need.

Consequences Novel

Dark Consequences

Cruel Consequences

Fatal Consequences

Haunting Love Novel

Third Time's the Charm

Thirteen Days Gone

One Mistake Too Late

Holiday Romance Novel

Merry Me

Mistletoe Magic

Christmas Wish

Snowed in Love

Snowflakes and Shots

Holiday Hope

Sleigh All the Way

Lucky Town Novel

Escaping Memories

Dangerous Memories

Stolen Memories

Deadly Memories

Forgotten Memories

McCord Family Novel

Protecting You

Trust in Love

Deserving You

Always Kind of Love

Finding You

Dare You to Love

Mona & Mason

The Paranormal Chronicles, Volume I

Perfect For You Novel

The Wrong Brother

The Right Time

The Easy Part

The Hard Choice

Psychic Love Novel

Exploding Love

Captured Love

Slaying Love Novel

Won't Let You Go

Doomed Love

Deadly Crazy

Evidence of Sin

Finding Redemption

Obsessed Hope

Short Stories

Paint By Murder

Follow Me, Sweet Darling

Sleighville Novel

Dashing Through the Fear

Here Comes Chaos

The Last Noel

Standalone Novel

The Danger with Love

Conquering Fear Novel

Co-written with Jane Blythe

Drowning in You

Out of the Darkness

Closing In

1

SHE DIDN'T LOOK over her shoulder as she walked with quick, meaningful strides, her purse tucked securely to her side. Her car sat across town, nowhere near the train station. No need to give any clues about how she fled town. After taking multiple buses and then hopping in a taxi, she asked to be dropped off five blocks from the destination she was nearly upon.

Had it all been enough?

Only time would tell.

Her hands shook as she dug in her purse for her wallet, her small duffle bag strapped across her chest. She had only packed what would fit in it. Everything else she had left behind. Not that she cared about anything she left behind. Useless objects that filled the space.

The attendant who sold her a ticket didn't blink an eye. Barely even looked at her as they took her money and then handed her a one-way ticket to St. Louis. Good. The fewer eyewitnesses, the better. She had even purchased a blonde wig to cover her auburn locks and added glasses that she didn't need to wear to see.

She didn't bother putting her duffel bag above the seat. Instead chose to keep both her purse and the bag clutched on her lap as the train took off. According to her ticket, it would take her three days to get to St. Louis from Orlando. Three stops total. When she hit her first stop in Washington, D.C. roughly eighteen hours later, she got off and didn't look back once.

Sure, she wasted money buying a ticket to a destination she never had any intention of going to, to begin with. But anything to knock someone off-balance if they managed to find a small clue of where to look for her.

After walking several blocks from the station, she hailed a cab and asked to be dropped off at the closest hotel. Lucky for her, there was a salon right across from it. The wig was starting to make her itch, and she didn't trust herself not to mess up dying her hair. She managed to get in right away and walked out as a true blonde. She'd keep the glasses for the time being. Instead of renting a room as the cabbie most likely had expected, she caught a bus until she saw a dealership.

She bought her first car ever. It wasn't much to talk about, but it would get her from point A to point B. No more spending money on useless destinations. Now, she could get to her last stop in a straight shot. It was silly how giddy she was at the prospect she'd picked this car herself. The other one she had owned had never been her style, one she hadn't even picked out herself. That was her old life. The one where she shut up and did as she was told. From here on out, every decision would be because it was what *she* wanted. Not what someone else wanted.

She drove to Pennsylvania then through Ohio and Indiana. Once she hit Illinois, instead of turning toward Wisconsin, she stayed straight to Iowa, then moved up to

Minnesota. Four days later, she was two towns away from the end of her journey.

She didn't want it to seem odd driving into town with nothing but a small duffle bag. A quick stop at a local mall solved the problem. She shopped so much her feet hurt and purchased so much that she ended up carrying bag after bag to her car. Clothes, toiletries, paintings, and wall decor that honestly held no meaning, but she'd pretend they did. Kitchen supplies, bedding, and some books because she couldn't wait to relax and simply read. Of course, to make it all appear legit, she found boxes as well and packed all the new belongings as if it were how she left her old home. No need to raise suspicions.

Had she done enough to make herself look innocent? She could only hope so. There was no turning back now.

When she got behind the wheel of her car, she sat there, gripping it. Wondering if she had done the right thing. The smart thing.

If he found her...

Nope. She would not think of it. Because it would do no good. She had left, and that was that. Her chance to change her mind had left the moment she ditched her car and never looked back.

She blew out a small breath and put the car into drive, plugging her final destination into the GPS she had purchased when she bought the car. She had no smartphone so couldn't use that device. That had been the first thing she'd gotten rid of when she left the house. No need to give him the ability to track her. Her car was so old it didn't even have windows that rolled down automatically. But this was the start of a new beginning. Eventually, she'd get all those fancy gadgets and be like everyone else. But first, she had to settle into her new life and find a job. The cash she'd snatched before leaving was dwindling to nothing.

Her eyes widened when she saw the welcome sign.

Welcome to Sleighville. Where you are sure to have a holly, jolly time.

God, she hoped so. Anything was better than the hell she'd been living in.

Though, as she saw the first tree all dolled up in ornaments and lights, she wondered if she hadn't traded one hell for another.

Her foot let up on the gas as she trailed through the main street of town, wincing at it all. Garland hung up in window shops. Christmas lights sparkling in every display. And the large sleigh carrying Santa with eight reindeer pulling it in the center of town made her want to puke.

When she pulled onto her street to the house she had rented, the same nauseating sight was everywhere. Lights strung up on gutters. Christmas paraphernalia set up in the yard from Santas to Frosty to elves that looked way too merry in her opinion.

But the house she pulled into sat bare. A quaint little house that almost looked like a gingerbread house. Square in design with a steeple roof. All it needed was some colorful gumdrops and icing sprinkled everywhere. It sat back from the other houses on the street, near the woods nestled behind it. Hiding from everything. That's exactly what she needed. To hide.

There hadn't been many options when she called to rent a place. When she finally decided she'd had enough, that if she didn't leave she'd die, she knew she had to flee somewhere he'd never look.

A town that celebrated Christmas year-round.

And as someone who hated Christmas—despised it with every breath in her body—she figured that would be the last place he'd think to look for her.

She got out of her vehicle, stretched her neck, and looked around. She had ditched the glasses before she hit Minnesota, so when the car pulled in right behind her, she felt naked and unprepared. She took a step back, ready to run.

Keep your cool. Don't act like a skittish ninny.

With that reminder in place, she greeted the woman who exited her vehicle with a cheery smile. Way too cheery, as if she *loved* celebrating Christmas year-round.

"Welcome to Sleighville! We're so happy to have you here. I'm Mindy. You must be Eve. We spoke on the phone."

She forced herself to put on a smile she didn't feel and stepped forward, shaking Mindy's hand. The woman gave her no choice as she kept it in the air waiting for her to move closer.

"Nice to meet you." She knew that came out strained and berated herself for not sounding more pleasant. "It's a lovely house."

It was, only it wasn't something she would've picked if she had a choice. Too close to Christmas cheer in her opinion. Why did it have to be shaped like a gingerbread house?

"Isn't it though!" Mindy clapped her hands, beaming with pride at the obnoxious building. "You'll love it." Her eyes glided to her car. "Do you have a moving truck coming later? I can have my brother Mark come and help you unpack. He's great about helping me with so much."

"Oh no. This is it. I don't like clutter." That was as good an excuse as any.

"So, Eve." Mindy headed up the walkway, waving her

hand for her to follow. "Is that short for Evelyn? It's such a pretty name. I went to school with an Evelyn. She moved to California to pursue an acting career. She hasn't hit it big yet, but she's still working the grind."

According to her new license, social security card, and one credit card she applied for, her full name was simply Eve Johnson. In reality, her real name was Evelyn Carrington. She'd changed her last name to something so common it would make it impossible to find her. She worried about messing up a new first name, so decided to stick with her name but shortened. He never liked it when people called her Eve either. Evelyn, Evelyn, Evelyn was all he ever tolerated, and for that reason alone, she hated her first name. Hopefully, the new ID she purchased from a very sketchy man in a dark alley a week ago held up. Her hands shook the entire time, and she knew the guy saw it when she handed over the money. But whatever. It was done, she had a new identity and there was no going back.

"No, it's just Eve."

Mindy tilted her head as if waiting for her to continue, make a comment about the other Evelyn who moved to California. What was she supposed to say to that?

"Wonderful. Eve is such a pretty name too."

Then they were off. Mindy opened the door and handed her the key, then gave her a quick tour of the house. There wasn't much to see. A small living room to the left with the dining room and kitchen to the right. If one could call it a dining room. More like a nook. Just off the kitchen down a tiny hallway was the bathroom and one bedroom. It was all absolutely perfect. It fit her so well. She didn't need much. A place to sleep and feel safe.

She managed to get Mindy to leave thirty minutes later,

which was saying something. The woman loved to talk. About anything and everything.

All she wanted to do was lay her head down for a moment and rest. Of course, she couldn't do that with nothing in the house. She didn't even have a bed!

But she had a pillow and blankets she purchased and that would have to do until she bought some furniture. While she had money for this adventure, she had to watch how she spent it. At least until she found a job somewhere.

Time to unpack her meager belongings. She opened the door and ran right into a solid wall. Except this wall had hands and grabbed her around the arms. She tensed, waiting for the blow. For the force of the fist or the jolt of the shove that would send her tumbling to the ground. She couldn't even open her eyes to see how much she was a failure. All that trouble to escape only to land right back into his hands. She knew she wasn't smart enough to get away. He told her all the time how pathetic she was. She'd proven him right.

GRIFFIN SENSED HER FEAR IMMEDIATELY. It wasn't hard to decipher with the way her eyes slammed shut and her shoulders cowered inward.

He made sure she was steady on her feet before letting her go and stepping off the lone step and to the pathway.

"I am so sorry. I was about to knock when you opened the door. Are you okay?"

The woman's eyes popped open in surprise as if she had expected someone else. The fear ebbed away.

"Oh, yes. I'm the one who's sorry. I wasn't watching where I was going."

He grinned. "I'm glad I didn't knock you down. Not the best way to welcome you to town."

"Are you part of some welcoming committee?"

The horror in her eyes at the prospect made him want to laugh. He figured that wouldn't go over well, and he was already on shaky ground with the near knocking her over incident.

"No," he said with a short chuckle because he couldn't resist. "We're neighbors." He pointed to the house on the right. It was hard to see the entire thing as her house was set back farther than his. Add in the trees, it hid the house very well. "I saw the car in the driveway and thought I'd say hi. Welcome you to Sleighville. If you need help moving your stuff, I'd be happy to help."

Her eyes darted to her car which was filled to the brim. Then she bit her bottom lip as if she were unsure if she should accept his friendly invitation. And that's all he was being—friendly. A neighborly gesture.

"Oh, geez. I didn't even introduce myself. I'm Griffin Stuart. I swear I'm harmless." He reached forward to shake her hand.

Her eyes bulged when she saw the firearm holstered on his hip, hiding under the loose jacket he had on. Spring had sprung and May was here, but it didn't mean the weather was totally pleasant yet. When he was off duty, he didn't like his weapon displayed for all to see either. But he didn't go anywhere without his service weapon.

He dropped his arm when she didn't return the handshake.

"I should also add I'm the chief of police of Sleighville. Hence, the weapon." He widened his smile to hopefully ease the worry in her eyes.

She nodded, then held out her hand in a very delayed reaction. He made no comment about it but shook her hand.

"Sorry, it surprised me. I guess I picked the right house. Can't beat having the chief of police next to me. I'm Eve."

"That's true." He laughed, even though her joke came out strained. "Nice to meet you, Eve. Would you like help unloading?"

"Oh, you don't have to. It's not much."

"I don't mind."

Maybe he shouldn't be so persistent with how skittish she appeared, but he couldn't help himself. She was a puzzle, and he could never resist a puzzle.

"Ok, sure."

She unlocked the car and grabbed a small duffle bag from the passenger seat, then opened the backseat and grabbed a box. He followed suit. They had the car unpacked in record time.

"Let me know when the moving van gets here, and I can help with that as well."

"This is it. But thank you."

He eyed the few boxes and bags in the empty living room. Odd. Not a lot of belongings. Where was the furniture? She had none.

"Well, if you need anything, I'm right next door. I work days, with a few odd nights here and there, but I'm around. It's a small town."

"I appreciate it."

Then she ushered him to the door and closed it before he could say anything else.

Very odd woman.

He'd keep his eye on her. Which wouldn't be too much

of a hardship. Long blonde hair, green cat-like eyes. Kissable lips. His steps faltered. No, he shouldn't be thinking about her lips and placing his mouth on hers. New in town and skittish. That was a recipe for disaster.

He walked across the lawn to his house, disarming the alarm before giving his cat, Walter, a few rubs on the back. He'd found the mangy thing digging in the trash behind the cafe. When he brought it to the shelter and it sat there for more than two weeks, no one coming to claim him, he took him home for himself. The pour guy looked pitiful with his one eye and front paw half gone. One of the volunteers, Timmy, had named him Walter, and Griffin hadn't the heart to change it. The cat did act like an old soul half the time and Walter fit him well.

"How was your day? You didn't get too crazy with the catnip, did you?"

Walter eyed him with a stony stare as if appalled he'd ask such a question. The cat had toys all over the house, catnip in every one. He'd yet to touch one of them. Such a waste of money.

Five fifteen.

Juliet would still be at the cafe, and Bryce would be heading out of the office soon himself. He chose to call Bryce. Though he was close to both of his siblings. They were the best of friends and had been since childhood.

"Want to grab a pizza and come over tonight?"

"Sorry, can't. Denise wants to *talk*."

Which was code for Bryce's wife wanted to lay into him for something that she had no right to. The woman nitpicked everything he did. Griffin still wasn't sure why he married the witch.

"Why, what's up?"

It wasn't uncommon for them to get together over a slice

or two. Sometimes Chinese, or takeout from Vinnie's Diner. Best meatloaf that was ever made. But Bryce knew him well, just as he knew his brother well.

"I met my new neighbor. She's...nice."

Bryce's laughter filled the entire room as if he stood right there with him. "Oh, I'll have to meet her soon. Where does she hail from? And what's her favorite thing about Christmas? I hope it's not elves. Those little bastards all lined up in Mr. Thorn's yard creep me out."

Griffin would agree with that assessment.

"I didn't ask. Either question. She didn't seem to want my company. Not quite standoffish, but not completely friendly."

More laughter spilled out. "Well, she moved to the wrong town then. I give it a month and that lovely cottage next to you will be empty once again."

Griffin almost took that bet but stopped himself. There was something about her. Until he put his finger on what that was, he wouldn't make any bets.

The house next to him had been a revolving door. Too many new tenants in the last year. Eight to be exact. Eve made it number nine. He didn't know what was wrong with the place. Maybe it was cursed.

"I gotta go, man. Let's grab lunch tomorrow."

Griffin agreed and hung up. He grabbed himself a beer, popped the top, and threw it in the trashcan under the sink. With his kitchen toward the back of his house, his window gave him a great view of her house. Right where her bedroom was. She had no curtains, so he could see her carrying a large bag into the room. The frown that marred her face made his heart skip a beat. Made the protective instincts he was born with flare to life.

His new neighbor was hiding something.

Something that frightened her.

It was his job to serve and protect, and that's exactly what he planned to do. Whether she liked it or not.

2

THE FIRST THING on the agenda—besides her morning coffee—was to find the nearest store that sold curtains. It hadn't occurred to her when she bought supplies at the mall to grab curtains. She had spied her neighbor once while he was doing something in his kitchen. He hadn't been in there long, so she knew he wasn't cooking. When she realized he could turn and spot her staring at him, she fled her bedroom. It had been a long, sleepless night of tossing and turning on her floor knowing he could see into her room. That *anyone* could see into her room.

So yes, curtains were the first thing on her to-do list for the day. The second thing would be to find a job.

She had spent all day yesterday unpacking and putting away the few belongings she had. By eight o'clock she'd been done and had nothing to do but read a book. The journey had been exhausting, so that hadn't lasted long, falling asleep on the hard ground. Maybe she'd add find a bed to her list today as well.

Around eight o'clock a knock on her door had her jumping, hating herself for the reaction. If she was going to blend in, then she needed to keep calm at all times.

She opened the door to a young man who wore a gentle grin and kind eyes.

"Sorry to bother you so early. Mindy said you arrived yesterday. Welcome to Sleighville. I'm Teddy and I live a few houses down the street. If you need anything, especially your lawn mowed, I'm your guy. At least for the summer. I start college in the fall."

Well, this was unexpected. The offer to mow her lawn, and the fact a teenager already knew she had arrived. Note to self: watch what she said to Mindy, who obviously loved to gossip and spread any kind of news.

"That's...very kind of you." She had no lawn mower and had never mowed a lawn in her life. "I'll take you up on that offer."

Teddy's smile widened. "Great. You have a wonderful day, Ms. Johnson. I'll be by next weekend to mow."

Eve waved good-bye, watching as he strolled down her pathway with merry steps. She hadn't even needed to tell him her name. She wasn't sure what to think about everyone knowing everything about her without ever meeting them before.

An hour later, she locked her door and drove her new car around town. When she entered the general store that seemed to have anything she wanted, she wanted to turn around and walk out. The Christmas music blaring through the speakers sent a chill down her spine. She ignored it as best as she could, grabbing a few curtains without paying much attention to the colors. It honestly didn't matter. As long as she had something to block the windows.

She tossed the bags into her car before deciding she'd walk down the main street and get a closer look at things.

Her steps slowed when she neared the cafe, her lips widening into a grateful smile.

Help wanted. Need a friendly, energetic person to maintain the front counter.

Eve was friendly. Energetic? Well, when she needed to get stuff done, she could pull out the energy without blinking. But with people, she was not so great. Again, she wanted to twirl around and walk out when the Christmas music blared through the speakers. Did every store play the dreaded tunes? That would get old real quick.

But she needed a job, and she'd endure whatever she had to to survive. Right now, she was in survival mode.

"Hi, welcome to Noel's Cafe. What can I get you?" the upbeat woman behind the counter asked.

She had long brown hair pulled into a chaotic ponytail with a black apron strapped around her body that read "Noel's Cafe" with a twig of holly. Her smile was beaming and her voice had a merry tune. Eve hesitated to ask about the position if she had to work next to a peppy, overly-happy person like her.

But she needed work.

"I was wondering about the help sign. Is there a manager I can speak with? I'm Eve." She made sure to brighten her smile as much as the woman's. Hers definitely was fake. Not like the woman across from her.

"You got her!" The woman held out her hand. "I'm Juliet. I own the cafe. Do you have any experience working in customer service?"

Her entire life felt like she'd been in customer service. Always on display, making sure no one had anything to complain about. *The customer was always right.* She nearly rolled her eyes as the thought slipped through her mind.

Though she hated being the center of attention and

mingling with people if she didn't have to, she had worked in a bakery that she loved. Creating works of art with her hands had been her passion. While she'd been behind the scenes most of the time, she'd dealt with customers on occasion. She knew how to handle people if forced to.

The problem was she couldn't exactly give references to her old job. That would lead back to her old life. While she had purchased a new identity, it hadn't come with a background in anything. She had a spiel ready for her lack of prior employment. Of course, she wanted to avoid that at all costs. She wasn't the best liar. Her poker face could use some work.

"Not really, but I'm a quick learner, and I like helping people."

Which wasn't exactly a lie. She liked to bake and help people eat wonderful treats.

"Great. You're hired. Come around the counter and I'll show you how to use the register."

Eve's mouth dropped open, eyeing the woman as if she'd lost her mind. Seriously, had she? She was going to hire her on the spot. No asking for references. No asking for her ID or anything. Not even fill out an application. She wanted to be grateful she didn't have to go into her fake spiel, but this felt odd.

But beggars also couldn't be choosers and she didn't have any other options on her plate.

"Okay, thank you."

Eve tried to wipe the surprise from her face as she walked around the counter.

"I'm not insane hiring someone I just met. You're Eve Johnson. You moved into town yesterday and live right next to the chief of police. It's a small town. Word gets around quickly. How do you like the house?"

"It's perfect."

That wasn't a lie either. She had a roof over her head and enough space to live a quiet life. She was coming to learn, though, not in the shadows. Not if Juliet already knew so much about her, that might be a problem. She had never considered that moving to such a small town everyone would get into everyone's business. She needed to stay under the radar. It was crucial to her survival. But she shouldn't be surprised. Teddy knew about her too.

"Don't worry. You'll get used to our little town. Come on. I'll show you where to stash your purse, and then I'll give you a crash course on how to run the counter."

Crash course it was. Juliet barely had time to show her how the register worked before a line formed. Lunchtime was a hopping time in the cafe.

"I'll have the BLT with some coleslaw."

Eve attempted a decent smile at the man with shaggy brown hair and sweat lingering on his forehead. When she handed him the food, dirt was packed underneath his nails and covering his hands. Construction worker? Carpenter? Definitely someone who worked hard labor, but the least he could do was wash his hands.

She gave him the total and tried not to cringe when he passed her a ten, touching her hand.

"Do I know you? I mean, you're Eve Johnson, just moved into the cottage, but have we met before? I'm Bob Taylor."

"We haven't."

He eyed her critically, his stare unnerving her. There was no way he recognized her from her former life. She'd made sure to change her appearance from her hair to the way she dressed.

"You look so familiar." He snapped his fingers, making her flinch. "I probably saw you driving into town. That must be it. I was working the sign yesterday when you drove through the road construction."

A silent breath released. That would make sense. She had no words to offer him though as the terror still ran through her veins.

"Have a great day, Eve."

She offered a weak smile, then greeted the customer behind him. The day dragged on with person after person.

"You look wiped. First day and Juliet is already pushing you to the limit."

She had no idea who this man was, but she wasn't going to say one bad word about Juliet. At the moment, the woman was her savior for giving her a job on the spot.

"What would you like to eat?"

The man's lips twisted into a crooked grin. "The daily special. Sorry. I'm sure everyone has been in your face all day. New in town and all."

"It's been...different." She had no idea how to describe people knowing who she was without even introducing herself, including this guy.

One bowl of chicken wild rice and a baguette roll—the daily special. The soup smelled wonderful. Her stomach even growled when she pushed the bowl closer to his side.

He handed her a twenty.

"I'm Duke, by the way. If you need anything, let me know."

She wouldn't, but the offer was nice. He wore a police uniform, so she could only assume he meant in the official capacity. Though his sweet grin could also mean he meant in a friendlier way than she was prepared for. She handed him his change, nodding with a smile. Not to encourage him, but because she needed to be polite. Acting any other way might raise his suspicions, and she already lived next to the chief of police. The last thing she wanted was to be on the radar of every officer in town.

Eve didn't get a break until two hours later when the line finally disappeared.

She felt sweat gathering in her armpits and her hair making her neck hot as well. After digging for a hair tie in her purse, she pulled her hair into a ponytail, just like Juliet. Now she knew to do that before she came to work.

While she manned the counter, ringing customers' purchases and re-stocking the displays of sweets and mini sandwiches, Juliet worked alongside Chip baking in the back area. Tabitha worked the tables, clearing them off, cleaning them, and making sure the people who stayed to eat never wanted for anything.

She heard the bell ring, indicating someone had stepped inside. She twisted her gaze to the door, pasting on her smile, forcing herself not to lose it when the last man she wanted to see stepped inside.

Griffin walked to the counter with the same smooth grin he had worn yesterday when he insisted he help her unload her car.

"Good afternoon, Eve. I see you found employment."

"Yes, Juliet was kind enough to hire me." On the spot, though she left those words out. It still sounded insane.

"I'm glad she found someone as fast as she did. The other woman who worked here just up and left. Didn't give a warning or anything. Really put Juliet on the spot."

Was he cautioning her not to do the same thing? Because while he kept that damn smile on his face, his tone held a slight bite. As if he suspected she was hiding something. Hiding from someone.

Well, tough. If she had to suddenly flee in the middle of the night, she would. She'd do whatever she had to to stay safe.

"I'm sorry to hear that. What can I get you, Chief?" Eve forced the merriness into her tone.

His eyes sparkled with mischief, his grin inching up further. "I insist you call me Griffin. We are neighbors, after all. I'll have one of the tuna sandwiches with a Danish."

"Of course."

She dashed to get his stuff and get him out of the cafe as quickly as possible. Then Juliet came out of the kitchen and ruined it.

"Grif! I'm so glad you stopped by. I need help moving one of my refrigerators."

He groaned. "Stop reorganizing the back. It looks fine the way it is."

"But it would work so much better on the opposite wall."

Eve suppressed a laugh when she saw he wanted to roll his eyes. "I told you that last week when you wanted to move it from that spot. Now you want to move it back."

"Well, I didn't know until I tried it in the other spot. Now I know."

He didn't look amused. Eve braced for his rage to emerge. She even took a step back, shielding her body with her arms wrapped around her middle. Then his lips twisted into a silly grin as laughter fell out.

"It wouldn't kill you to say you were right, Grif. You. Were. Right. Three simple words."

Juliet pursed her lips in a comical way, making eye contact with Eve. "Men wanting to hear those elusive words." Then she busted out laughing. "Not going to happen. Eat your food and meet me back there." She started to walk away, then looked at Eve one more time. "If my brother ever acts like an idiot, let me know. I'll set him straight."

Then she left the area.

Brother.

Juliet and Griffin were siblings.

Wow. Just great. Her entire life was getting intertwined with two of the most outgoing, outspoken people in the town. Or maybe there was something in the water. Mindy had been a chatterbox too.

"Is Mindy your sister too?"

Griffin flinched at the question, his brows drooping. "What?"

Her cheeks burned as she realized that was a rude question. Why blurt it out as she had? What did it matter?

"Nothing." She pushed his food closer to his side. "Here you go. That'll be seven ninety-five."

He handed her a ten, eyeing her with a critical stare. She hated it. The last thing she needed was the chief of police keeping an eye on her.

She broke the law!

She was living in town with a fake identity.

Her hands shook despite trying to keep her cool as she handed him the change. His fingers brushed hers, causing her eyes to dart to his. The touch had been brief but electrifying. Nothing like when she touched Bob's hand. He didn't appear to be affected by it, but his gaze was still intense. She'd never felt such a shock by a simple touch—from anyone.

"Thanks, Eve." He tossed the change into his pocket, then grabbed his food. "Mindy isn't my sister. I'm sure you'll meet Bryce at some point. He's the mayor of the town and my brother. We were supposed to have lunch today, but he cancelled on me. My parents moved to Arizona a few years back. A few aunts, uncles, and cousins sprinkled around town too. That's my family in a nutshell. Do you have any siblings?"

So many odd things about her, and he wanted to figure every part of her out. Part of it was the cop in him. Part of it was simple curiosity. He could never resist a puzzle. Which some would suggest always came back to the cop in him.

"Only child."

The way she pressed her lips together, her eyes avoiding his gaze, he figured she lied to him.

Why?

Over such an innocent question.

"Well, if you ever wondered what growing up with siblings is like, you'll get a great picture working for Juliet. She will be like your annoying older sister. In your business. Bossing you around. Nitpicking this and that."

She winced at his description. Now that he thought about it, that wasn't a pretty picture of his sister. He hadn't meant it in a bad way. Only that once Juliet accepted you into her life, she was hard to get out of it. In a good way, of course. How did he explain that properly?

"She is the boss. Bossing me around is part of the package."

"Right." He shifted the plate of food to his other hand. "I didn't mean to make her sound mean. She's not. She's wonderful to work for. I meant she'll be there for you."

"Thank you."

She didn't sound like she meant it, and he honestly couldn't blame her.

"And you get me as an older brother. It's like having a family you didn't ask for."

Her eyes rounded, her frown turning more severe.

Yes. He understood that as well. He was digging himself further and further into a hole he had no idea how he found himself in.

When she didn't say anything, he lifted his plate. "Thanks for the food."

She eyed him funny but nodded without saying anything.

He walked away before he said anything else stupid. The table near the window was open, so he snatched it. He liked to keep an eye on things outside while also having a nice view of everything in the cafe. He had a clear line of sight to the front door. And Eve as well.

The way she moved rigidly behind the counter told him she was on edge. Because of him? Because that was her normal behavior? He'd find out soon enough. Because he wouldn't be able to help himself.

The food disappeared quickly, and he realized he didn't purchase anything to drink. So back to the counter he went. Not a hardship at all because he was enjoying the view in front of him.

"Oh!" Eve sputtered when she turned around from the back counter to see him waiting patiently for her.

She'd been digging for napkins in the cupboard, and he had enjoyed the view of her ass in the air. Maybe a little too much. For a woman with too many secrets, he needed to keep his distance. Not to mention she lived in the cursed house. His luck, he'd get to know her, fall for her, and she'd skip town like every other resident before her who'd lived in that house.

"Can I help you with something else?" she asked when he stood there like an idiot saying nothing.

"Oh, right. I forgot a drink." He leaned over to the cooler filled with various bottles of pop and water and snatched the largest bottle of water they sold. "This will do."

"How was the food?"

Though the question came out with a smile, he sensed she had to force it out.

"Delicious, as always. Have you tried the food here yet?"

She shook her head, then rattled off the price.

He handed her a five and held out his hand for his change. The devil hidden inside him made sure her fingers grazed his hand once again. The short spark he had felt the first time ignited again. Her eyes rounded in large saucers as if she had felt the same electrical charge.

"Juliet is great about employees taking some of the left-over food that doesn't sell home. Grab a tuna sandwich if there is any left. The rest she brings to the homeless shelter."

The first real smile brightened her face. "That's a wonderful thing to do. I'd rather the food go to them."

He sensed she meant that. She might have secrets she didn't want to share, but she had a kind soul. That's all that mattered to him. She could keep her secrets—as long as it didn't involve breaking the law.

He returned a gentle smile, grabbed his water, and said good-bye before heading to the back of the cafe. Juliet was rolling dough and singing to Rudolph that was blaring out of the speakers.

"So you hired the newbie in town?"

Juliet looked up from her worktable, her eyes sparkling

with merry. "She's great. Been working her butt off ever since I pulled her behind the counter. You said she seemed harmless."

Griffin groaned. While he had chatted with Juliet briefly last night about his new neighbor, he didn't think she'd take that as a glowing review to hire her. Not that Griffin thought it was a bad idea. As long as Juliet did her due diligence. Which he suspected she hadn't.

"You at least called a reference or two?"

Juliet averted her eyes, putting more muscle into the rolling pin.

"Seriously, Jules."

Her eyes narrowed. "Hey, I don't nitpick how you do your job, so don't do it to me. It's all good. I like her. And if you had any suspicions about her you should've said so last night."

"I don't really."

"But?" Juliet drawled.

"But nothing. She seems like a nice woman who just moved into town. With barely any belongings, skittish behavior, and too many fake smiles. She's hiding something, and I want you to be aware of who you're hiring. The last lady left without even a damn good-bye."

The room went silent at that. Chip paused from taking some pies out of the oven, and Juliet froze with her arms outstretched with the rolling pin.

"Beth was flaky from the beginning. I should've known better than to hire her. I have a good feeling about Eve." She rolled the pin back her way. Chip continued in his quest of the pies. "I know what you're talking about. She also likes to keep her space from others. Classic signs of abuse. I should know."

Griffin's teeth clenched at the reminder. The bastard

who had hurt Juliet was sitting in prison doing ten years. Not long enough in his opinion. What hurt more than knowing someone had hit her was knowing how long he had physically abused her. That Juliet let him do it one too many times. Though she hadn't allowed it to the point he killed her, so there was that. His sister was one of the strongest women he knew. While it gutted him she hadn't turned to him right away, she had eventually, that's what counted.

If their suspicions were correct about Eve—because he agreed with Juliet's assessment—then Griffin only had to be patient with Eve as well.

She'd tell him her secrets.

Because he wouldn't have it any other way.

When someone moved to his town, they became part of his family, his community, and he took his job seriously. No one would harm her on his watch. It also didn't hurt he found her very attractive. Those eyes of hers reeled him in with little effort.

"It's going to take a while for her to open up about anything."

Juliet cocked a brow. "And don't go pushing her about it either. Leave her alone."

Griffin held up his hands in an innocent gesture. "I would never. You know that. But keep your eyes peeled for anything odd. You see something suspicious, I want to know. She's here and that makes her part of our community."

Juliet held up the rolling pin like she meant to use it as a weapon. "And no one messes with our merry community."

"Ho, ho, ho," Chip cheered from the other counter, holding up the knife he'd been using to cut the pie into slices.

Griffin chuckled, setting his water on the counter. "Now

let's take care of this refrigerator. Make sure this is where you want it because I'm not moving it again."

Juliet pointed to the contraption, the devil dancing in her eyes. Which meant if it had to be moved again, he'd be moving the damn thing. Because he loved his sister and would do anything for her.

Same went for anyone else in town—Eve included.

3

SHE STRETCHED TO THE RIGHT, trying to undo the kink in her lower back that had settled there the past three days. That's what happened when one slept on the hard floor with nothing between their body to protect them. She needed a bed. A proper one. Unfortunately for her, they didn't have much to choose from.

Who knew that when a person moved to a town that celebrated Christmas year-round they took that motto seriously? Too seriously.

The three different versions of sleigh bed frames that peered back at her said as much. She didn't want to sleep in a bed that looked like Santa might jump in and fly away into the night sky.

She couldn't even believe that they had three different types of sleigh-like beds either. One was plenty.

But she had to pick one because she'd already asked for just a bedframe and apparently they didn't sell those. It was merriment or nothing.

"You look deep in thought."

Eve shrieked, placing a hand to her heart as she jumped, tripping on her feet. Griffin was lightning fast, grabbing her around the waist before she would've bonked her head on the very sleigh she hated to purchase.

Her body trembled as his warm arm wrapped around her, cocooning her in safety. She hated to admit to herself she wasn't trembling from the fright he'd given her but from his strong and gentle touch. No one had ever handled her so tenderly before.

"Are you okay? I didn't mean to startle you."

"I'm...I'm fine." She pulled a smile from nowhere, hoping that would appease him and he'd let her go. While she had no fear he'd harm her, she didn't like how he made her feel. She hadn't come to this town to fall into the arms of a man. Get trapped in a relationship. Worry about if she could trust him or not. Trust did not come easily to her, if it would at all. She'd never been able to trust anyone in her life.

He must've sensed her unease because he let her go, but not before making sure she was steady on her feet.

She took a step back, still reeling from his touch. No amount of retreating would put her at ease. Only when she couldn't see him would she feel better. Her body still felt electrified by his touch.

They stared at each other for the longest time, neither saying a word.

She didn't know what to say. Reacting the way she had was idiotic. She was supposed to be living under the radar, not making him look at her deeper with her silly reactions. This was the first time she'd seen him in the past few days since he ate at the cafe. She hadn't even seen him next door arriving or leaving, or through the window in his kitchen.

She'd hung up the curtains, the little protection they provided. That's what happened when she didn't pay attention to what she purchased—she screwed herself over. They were sheer curtains, letting prying eyes still pry. Even worse than that, they had dancing elves all over them. She had nightmares of elves dancing right off the curtains and attacking her in her sleep.

Before she left this store, she'd be leaving with more curtains—that would be blackout—and a mattress that would lay on the floor. She'd made her decision. No way was she buying a sleigh frame.

"So what one do you like best?" he finally asked, breaking the silence and their intense stare.

"You mean do I like the sleigh bed, the sleigh bed or," she said pointing to each one, "the sleigh bed? It's so hard to decide."

She hadn't meant to joke around with him. The faster she got out of his presence, the better, but when he laughed, it filled her heart with a bit of joy. Something she hadn't experienced in a very long time. If she really had experienced it. Her life had been nothing but disappointment and sorrow.

"I can see how it would be difficult to decide." He put a finger to his chin, pretending to ponder which one he'd pick as he looked at the frames. "I'd go with the sleigh bed."

She giggled, unable to control it. His gaze caught hers once again. The intensity of it frightened her. She tore her eyes away first.

"I think I'm going to just get a mattress. I never expected there wouldn't be many options to choose from."

"Most folks, if they want something non-Christmas related, shop out of town. These things are for the tourists and such. I can show you a great place two towns over."

Her eyes swiveled to his once again. They looked innocent enough. But could she trust him? Sit in a vehicle for any length of time and not give away how terrified she was?

And not necessarily that he'd hurt her. No. More along the lines of how he made her feel. Especially when he touched her.

"I don't need much. I would just like a frame. No headboard is necessary."

He nodded. "I can provide that. I have an old one sitting in the shed."

Her brows puckered. "Why? That's very odd to have lying around."

"Well, the house you're renting gets rented out a lot. Some people don't always take all their stuff. I have a lot of treasures sitting in the shed. You're welcome to browse through it all and take what you need."

Why did she feel like that was another subtle warning from him not to split town in the middle of the night?

"For a price?"

"As a neighborly gesture. Not everything has to come with a price."

Not in her world. Where she lived, everything always came at a price.

"I—"

His hand touched her shoulder, cutting off her words. He pulled it away when he noticed her flinch. She had to work on that.

"Eve, please take whatever you need. I've been meaning to take the stuff to a donation center. You'd be helping me out. Here I was helping Mindy out by storing the stuff, and I still haven't gotten rid of anything."

Somehow he managed to turn it around and make it seem like she'd be the one doing him a favor. It *would* help her save money. Something she desperately needed to do. The little amount of money she'd snatched before she left was nearly depleted, and she wouldn't get paid from the cafe for another few days.

"Okay. I appreciate it. I'll be over later tonight, if that's okay. I have an afternoon shift at the cafe and should be done a little after six after we clean up."

"I'll cook and have it ready by seven."

"Oh, that's not—"

"I'll see you then, Eve." He winked, cutting her off once again, then walked away before she could protest.

What just happened?

She didn't want to have dinner with him. Be in the same room as him. Pretend that everything was normal in her life. She only wanted to live in her bubble and forget all about her troubles. That was impossible to do when every time she looked at him she was reminded that he was the law. She broke it every day using the alias she purchased in a dirty alley.

While she waited for the clerk to ring up her supplies— curtains, bedsheets, a comforter, and a mattress—her mind swirled with excuses to get out of tonight's dinner.

Nothing good came to mind other than feigning a headache. Problem was she knew she was a terrible liar. She knew he already suspected something was off about her. She could see it in his eyes every time he glanced her way.

Her shift at the cafe went by fast. Juliet talked her ear off, as usual. Eve had no idea how she could be so chipper all the time. Displaying a smile every minute of the day. Her face hurt forcing a smile for most of her shift.

By the time she arrived home, she wanted nothing more than to take a shower and crawl under her blankets on the hard floor. Unfortunately, her mattress wouldn't be delivered for another two days.

Instead, she fixed the little makeup she wore, combed her hair, and put it back into the ponytail she had it in. She paused putting her lip gloss back into the medicine cabinet hiding behind the mirror.

Her lotion, toothpaste, and floss all sat on the bottom shelf, yet something didn't look right. She swore this morning she put the lotion bottle on the right side, and now it sat on the left. Or had she?

"Stop it, Eve!"

Shaking her head, trying to release all the tension filling her up, she put her mind back into focus. The lip gloss hit the middle shelf with a soft clink. She was losing her mind. Making things appear odd when in reality, she was afraid to walk across the lawn. She'd eat quickly, grab a few things from the shed, and leave. Nothing to worry about.

A few minutes later, she carried the half-consumed pie Juliet insisted she take home with her across the bright-green grass. Griffin opened the door before she could knock.

It startled her for some reason, causing her to step back —as usual, tripping on her feet—again.

GRIFFIN HAD a split second to decide whether to save the pie flying in the air or grab Eve before she went tumbling down two steps. Eve won.

He caught her arm, pulling her to him, wrapping his free hand around her waist. The position put her squarely in his arms, letting him inhale the lovely scent of vanilla. Her shampoo? Perfume? Or remnants from the cafe? He wasn't sure and he honestly didn't care. The smell was divine and made him ache to pull her even closer until his lips connected with hers.

But the tremble that touched her body had him releasing her instead. He needed to stop terrifying the woman. Why did it keep happening to him?

"I'm sorry. Again." A small grin touched his lips, hoping to dispel the fright still lingering in her eyes.

"I brought pie."

Their eyes glided to the gooey mess coating the grass near his porch steps.

"I bet it was delicious."

She laughed, making him relax. She wasn't angry with him.

"How does lasagna sound?" He gestured with his arms for her to enter. "I have Oreos for dessert in lieu of the pie."

"As long as you have milk so I can dunk them."

"Full gallon purchased today."

The tentative smile that splayed across her lips made the rest of the anxiety coursing through his skin disappear. She stepped by him and inside the house, sighing.

"Was that a good sigh or a bad one?"

She looked appalled that he heard her at all. "I'm so sorry."

"For what?" he asked, closing the door before she could escape.

He'd told himself for the past three days to forget about her. Let the mystery surrounding her be that—a mystery. He didn't need to solve every puzzle that landed in front of him. Of course, chatting with Juliet every night didn't help him, especially when she couldn't stop talking his ear off about Eve this and Eve that. It also hadn't helped that he'd seen her in her bedroom two nights in a row, changing for bed. The curtains she had purchased were a joke. They did nothing to hide the fact she had a body he wanted to touch from head to toe. His hands on her backside. His lips caressing her taut nipples. His cock—not thoughts he should be thinking at the moment.

Despite the many warnings to himself to leave her alone, he couldn't do it. He saw her in the store looking at bed frames and had to speak to her. Say hi. Somehow, the invite came out, and now here he stood wanting to push her against his foyer wall and kiss her until she begged him not to stop.

"Umm...for...I'm not sure I should be here."

He had to tread carefully. The last thing he wanted to do was frighten her so much she never spoke to him again. He could control his libido. He could keep his hands to himself. It didn't mean he wanted to, but he could.

She didn't need a man shoving his way into her life. What she needed was a friend. So that's what he'd give her. As long as he stopped scaring her to the point she tripped and having to catch her, he shouldn't have a problem keeping his hands to himself.

"I can show you the shed, and you can take a look at the things inside. While you do, I'll make your plate to-go. It's okay if you'd rather skip the meal." Then he waved a hand for her to follow.

He heard her steps behind him, so didn't bother to turn around. The click of unlocking the lock was the only sound that perforated the air around them. Then the creaking of the door as he swung it open. He stepped back to give her space.

"Whatever you want, it's yours."

She walked inside the shed.

"I was only trying to be friendly. Nothing else. You're safe here, Eve. In this town."

When she didn't turn around or acknowledge him, he headed back inside to prepare her food. It was better this way. As he had told himself earlier, the house next to him was cursed. The residents never lasted long, and putting his heart out there for her to stomp all over it wasn't wise.

He'd had it crushed once before, and that was one time too many.

Half the lasagna went into a container for her to take home, while the other half he shoved into his fridge. He'd eat later. If his appetite came back. How had the night turned so sour so fast?

Because he nearly knocked her down again? Because she didn't like the look of his house?

He had a small house. Two bedrooms, one bath. No Christmas paraphernalia anywhere inside, though he had lights hanging off his gutters and a Santa on his front porch. Tourists loved to see that. But inside his domain, he didn't need the holiday cheer shoved in his face. He had it every-where else in town to keep him merry.

Twenty minutes went by before she knocked on his sliding door. He gestured her in, putting the last dish in the dishwasher.

"Umm...you weren't kidding. It's like a room full of trea-sures. I feel bad taking anything."

Yes, he figured, but he'd insist because he knew her house was bare and that's what friends did. They helped each other when they needed it. He knew she wanted space from him, so he'd give it to her. He'd never force himself on anyone, even for friendship. But first, she had to take what she wanted from the shed.

"I want you to have whatever caught your eye. Please."

Perhaps it was the added please or the determination in his eyes, but she nodded, a sweet smile emerging.

"I'd love the dresser and the china cabinet. The table and chairs would be nice too. Of course, the bed frame. The small nightstand was pretty as well." She bit her lip, then added, "The two lawn chairs are nice and the table with the umbrella. I also liked the standing mirror."

He couldn't hold in his smile. "You didn't like the coffee table?"

A beautiful giggle escaped. "I did, but I don't have a couch yet and I can't picture a coffee table without the couch."

"I have a loveseat in the basement I never use. You can have it if you want."

She frowned, and he knew he'd overstepped again. She'd flee at any moment.

"Why are you so nice?"

He didn't know how to answer that. No one had ever asked such an odd question.

"Because my parents raised me well?"

She giggled again. "You don't sound sure about that."

"I don't know how to answer that. I like helping people. It's always been in my nature. It's one of the reasons I became a cop." He tossed a shoulder up. "Plus, I love solving puzzles."

She tensed at that, her eyes sparking with fear. As quickly as it appeared, she tried to cover it up.

Oh, yeah. She was a puzzle all right, one he was determined to ignore.

"Okay, I'll take the loveseat too."

He nodded, unable to hide his triumphant smile.

She looked down when Walter grazed her leg. "Oh, you have a cat."

Why did she sound so surprised? Did he not look like an animal person? Or just not a cat person? Before Walter, he wouldn't have considered himself a cat person, but the title fit him now. The house would feel empty without Walter roaming around.

"That's Walter. That means he likes you. Normally, he stays in his own space when people are around." He was not always a people person. Walter could be a grouch on occasion, especially with company.

Her eyes met his, another tender smile appearing. Then she gave Walter a few strokes on the back before standing up. She swallowed before speaking again. "Moving all that won't be easy. We should eat to build our strength. I'd like to try your lasagna. Here. If the offer still stands."

He knew getting to know her would be difficult, like walking on shaky ground with no safety in sight. But he'd always known that from the beginning. Nothing had changed. Except his attraction for her increased every time he touched her. So he'd stop touching her. Keep it strictly platonic and on friendly terms.

"Definitely. Have a seat and I'll grab us some plates."

He grabbed the lasagna from the fridge then, turning, he collided with her. His hands were full, so he was unable to catch her, though she wasn't so completely unsteady that she fell. Her hands caught his shoulders before she could.

"I'm sorry. I...I thought I could get by before you turned." She pointed at the sink. "To wash my hands."

Her fingers on his shoulders sent the desire straight to his cock, making him want to toss the container to the side and pull her into his arms. Kiss her like he had wanted to in the foyer. Except she pulled away from him, backing up a step.

Right.

No touching.

No kissing.

Friends only.

"I'll grab the plates."

"I'll wash my hands."

And he would think about baseball or something to reduce the bulge digging in his pants to be released.

How had he gone from wanting to figure her puzzle out to wanting to kiss her breathless?

4

"O-M-G!"

Eve jumped, and not because she feared someone was going to harm her. She twisted around to Juliet's delightful face.

"Sorry." Juliet looked contrite. "I didn't mean to scream in your ear. Girl, these cupcakes are too cute. You're so lucky you didn't hide this talent from me for long."

The happiness inside Eve wanted to burst free, but she held it in, settling for one of her short smiles.

"I'm so glad you like them."

"Love them. I *love* them."

Juliet swiped the tray of red, white, and blue cupcakes from the counter and headed for the front where she would fill in the spots already purchased.

The last month and a half had been some of the best days of her life. Eve couldn't remember a time she had been happier. Not even from her childhood. That wasn't anything to reminisce about.

After they had an awkward meal, Griffin had helped her move all the furniture from the shed to her house. The next day when he stopped in for lunch at the cafe, the weirdness lingered. It took a full week before they morphed into an easygoing friendship. He stopped in the cafe daily, either to say hi or to grab a bite to eat. Gone were the nerves. Gone were the worries. Gone was the apprehension. It was nice having a guy she could trust and rely on for once in her life. She didn't fear him in the slightest.

Well, not much.

When he touched her, which was rare these days, she feared how her body would react. Because his touch always sent the desire coursing through her veins. Just a brush of his fingers handing him change. Or the shift of their shoulders as they passed by each other in the kitchen when she had dinner with him or he had dinner at her house. The touches were so brief, yet so powerful, she made sure to avoid them at all costs.

Three weeks ago, Juliet had been in a pinch when Chip called out sick with the flu. She'd needed help in the back. Eve didn't hesitate to lend a hand, and ever since then, she'd been side by side with Chip baking as if she'd been hired to do so. She couldn't complain. She preferred being in the kitchen rather than behind the front counter. Less people to deal with. Some people asked too many questions. Her tongue got stuck at times on how to respond without drawing more suspicion than was already surrounding her. She knew some of the townsfolk eyed her funnily and she hated it.

While she detested making Christmas treats every day, she loved baking. Today, being the Fourth of July, she had created cupcakes with tiny little elves holding the American flag. By Juliet's beaming smile, she knew she loved them. Eve was proud of herself as well. She'd already baked her third batch of the day, and they were flying out of the cafe fast.

"You know she's going to have you making the cupcakes from now on, right?" Chip chuckled, bumping her hip.

She'd gotten used to him. He gave her no choice. He was a very touchy-feely guy but in an innocent way. He was always bumping her hip or wanting a high-five. She would've found it odd and uncomfortable, except he did the same to Juliet and Tabitha. She'd even braved bumping his hip a time or two, like yesterday when his timer for the pies went off and he didn't notice. A little bump to get him out of his thoughts and he was racing to the ovens.

She felt safe and comfortable in this town. A feeling she never thought she'd ever have. For the first time in her life, she felt like she belonged somewhere. She had a home, a community, and friends she could count on. Despite the few who stared a little too long at her sometimes, the worries inside dissipated a little more each day.

"I set the cupcakes out and five are already gone," Juliet said, stepping through the swinging doors. "Tabitha and I can barely keep up."

Though her laughter said she wasn't sorry about that at all.

"I'm glad they're a hit. Do you want me to make more?" It was already three o'clock in the afternoon. The cafe closed at six every day. Today they would be closing at five so everyone could join in the holiday festivities. It would take her at least an hour to bake and decorate more cupcakes, if not a bit longer.

"No, we're good for today. But you better start thinking of a great Labor Day idea. Those elves were amazing."

Labor Day.

A holiday still two months away and Juliet thought she'd

still be here. Eve hoped so. She hadn't felt eyes on her or anything, as if he had found her. She was safe. She was free. Though, she had odd moments here and there in her house when she felt like something was off. As if she had put something in one place and it somehow moved to another.

Or she was losing her mind, creating havoc when none was to be found.

Yes, Labor Day.

She would be here because she had escaped and he would never find her.

"I will start jotting down ideas tonight."

"No, you will not." Juliet pressed her lips together in a stern expression, but her eyes were lit up with joy. "You'll be having too much fun celebrating. You can't miss the fireworks."

She didn't like big crowds. Never had. Never would.

"I'm going to have a quiet night at home."

"You're coming out with me. That's final."

She didn't want to argue with Juliet, but she also didn't want to go out tonight. Not even Griffin had asked her to hang out tonight. Not that she expected him to ask her. They were only friends. Sure, they had dinner together once a week at one of their houses, but that was it. It was all platonic. Because they were only friends. If he had asked her, she would've told him no as well.

"Fireworks are not my thing."

Juliet frowned until Chip walked by her, bumping her hip.

"Not everyone likes crowds. You know it gets insane around here. She doesn't want to go, she doesn't want to go."

Juliet's frown increased as she watched Chip walk to the counter and grab a loaf of bread, tossing it into a bag and tying it shut. The food they didn't sell or use today would be dropped off at the homeless shelter. Eve enjoyed helping Juliet drop it off every night. Of course, some nights Chip did it, and other nights Tabitha did it. Eve hadn't yet done it on her own, but one of these days she would. If only they'd let her. She'd offered once, and Juliet told her no. No explanation, just no. Eve didn't have the guts to ask why.

"But we'll miss you there. Tabitha and I always go together, and we get the best spot. Griffin and Bryce have one right next to us. Of course, Denise will be there with him, and I think Griffin will have Melody there with him." Juliet rolled her eyes as if she didn't like the idea.

Eve had to agree. Since when was Griffin seeing someone? He never said a word. Not that he had to tell her everything, but he was usually very open and honest with her. Telling her things she had yet to have the bravery to talk about.

That sealed the deal for her as well. She didn't want to be around Griffin if he had a date. That would be hard to witness.

But they were only friends.

It would eventually happen. Him dating. She'd have to get used to it.

Juliet walked closer to her, pleading with her eyes. "Please, come with. Melody is not my favorite person and I need backup. Someone to help keep me in line so I don't claw her eyes out or something."

Eve snorted. "And you think I'm good backup? Have you lost your mind?"

"Some days, but today it's intact." Juliet smiled, garnering a chuckle out of her. "Griffin thinks you're coming. You have to be there."

But why would he need her there? He had his own date.

"Like Chip said, I'm not fond of crowds. I get..." Oh, what was a good word for that? "Um...claustrophobic, you know."

Juliet sighed. "You're sure I can't talk you into it?"

"I will be waiting with bated breath to hear all about it tomorrow morning. I'll even open the cafe up at six am for you. You can sleep in."

"Ha!" Juliet laughed. "I forgot how to sleep in, but I will let you open up. Those croissants you make melt in your mouth. I need some of those tomorrow. Your butt is making them."

"Deal."

And thank goodness that was the end of that.

"WHAT DO you mean Eve isn't coming tonight?" Griffin had to have heard Juliet wrong. Eve had to come. He wouldn't be able to endure Melody's obnoxious laugh all night without Eve's beautiful laughter counteracting it.

"She's not a fan of crowds, I guess. I thought you were going to ask her to come with. When she didn't mention it, I had to do it."

Well, he thought about it, and after a long hard night of thinking too much about it, he decided not to. They were friends. Things were easygoing between them. No awkwardness like that first night he invited her over. He didn't want to lose that. He enjoyed spending time with Eve. Getting to know her wasn't easy, navigating through questions as if he were walking in a minefield. If he asked the wrong one, the progress he made with her could come crumbling down in seconds. Asking her to the Fourth of July event could've been construed as a date, and he hadn't wanted to mess with the status quo. He had assumed she'd go with Juliet and he would've seen her there anyway. So much for assuming things.

"I assumed she'd come with you."

Besides hanging out with him on occasion, she had seemed to hit it off with Juliet. She talked nonstop about how wonderful Juliet was as a boss and a person, and Juliet rattled off the same tune about Eve.

"Well, she's not, you idiot. Instead of doing something, you're messing things up."

"What the hell does that mean?"

"Melody." Juliet huffed in his ear so loud he had to pull the phone away. "Why are you going with Melody tonight? You should be taking Eve."

"I'm not going with Melody." Griffin pinched the bridge of his nose, forcing the groan that wanted to escape to remain inside. "I don't know why you think that I am."

"Bryce said she was."

Griffin slammed his hand down on his desk. "I told Denise that if Melody wanted to tag along with her that was fine, but I wasn't picking her up or anything. I don't know how to be any more clear with those two that I'm not dating Melody."

"Have you tried actually saying those words to her?"

"Yes, Juliet, I've said it. The woman doesn't give up." He didn't even need to clarify which one because both Denise and Melody fit the bill.

"Okay, then you need to ask Eve to go with you."

He sighed. "You said she's not a fan of crowds."

"Griffin, I love you, but you're so dense sometimes. You like her. I suspect she likes you. Ask the woman out!"

The line went dead.

Great. His sister hung up on him and expected him to do something he told himself not to do.

While he'd be attending the fireworks tonight as a guest rather than on duty, he was still technically on duty. He wouldn't be able to sit there without roaming the crowd and making sure people behaved. It wasn't the best time to ask out anyone on a date.

The way things were going between them, he wasn't ready to ruin anything. He told himself that all the way until his shift ended and he was driving home. He reminded himself of it as he walked to his front door and a few times while he changed. He repeated it one more time before he found himself knocking on Eve's door.

She opened it wearing a T-shirt with a reindeer on it with the words *Wishing you a Merry Christmas* above the cheery creature. He knew Shannon from the tourist trap store near the cafe gave it to her. Shannon created holiday prints for everyone in town. First one was always on the house. Griffin had at least ten shirts hanging in his closet. Eve would soon join the rest of them by buying too many shirts she didn't need. Shannon just knew how to reel people in.

For pants, she had on a pair of sweats that looked two sizes too big for her. She looked adorable as hell, and he wished he could spend the night with her instead of a crowd that might get too rowdy. It happened on occasion. Every year was a toss-up whether it would be fun and games, or cuffs and sirens.

"Oh, hi, Grif. Happy Fourth of July."

She had started using the nickname most people used two weeks ago. He enjoyed hearing it every time she said it. Since her name was already short, he had nothing unique to call her. He was still thinking on it because he'd like a nickname for her.

"I thought I'd swing by and make sure you didn't want to come. Juliet said you're not a fan of crowds."

"No, sorry." Her gentle smile spoke the truth.

He'd come to learn her facial expressions. The smiles that he knew were fake and she wasn't necessarily lying to him, but she also wasn't being completely truthful. The smiles that said she truly loved something or hated it. The smiles that depicted she was enjoying herself or that she was ready to leave. She had a smile for everything, and he knew what each one meant.

"I wish I could stay with you. I'm not a huge fan myself."

"Really? That surprises me."

"Well, I guess it depends on the crowd. Fourth of July is a toss-up. Sometimes, it's great, and other times I have to pull out the handcuffs because some people don't know how to hold their liquor."

The worry line he saw every now and again when he spoke about his job appeared. "Be careful tonight."

"I always am. How about dinner tomorrow? I'll grill some steaks."

That beautiful smile he loved the most appeared. The one that bestowed the joy she couldn't hide.

"I'd like that. I'll make potato salad."

"Have a good night, Eve."

"You too, Grif."

He was halfway down her walkway when she hollered, "Be safe."

When he twisted to reassure her once again, the door was already closed. It was for the best. He might've caved and decided to stick around with her.

The festivities were hopping when he arrived. Vendors with food, games, and drinks were scattered around the grounds near the lake where the fireworks would go off.

Santa sat in the gazebo with a line of children waiting to sit on his lap. He tossed his blanket down next to Juliet's and Bryce's, smiling at Melody who stood near the cooler he knew was full of water and pop. He never drank at this event and neither did Bryce. Juliet would indulge, but she also didn't have to worry about crowd control.

"Hey, Grif. I almost thought you weren't coming."

He wasn't running too far behind schedule, but he had arrived later than he usually did. Eve had distracted him a little too much.

"Busy day. How are you, Melody?"

"Perfect." Her eyes glided to Bryce and Denise as they approached. Griffin swore her eyes lingered on Bryce longer than they should've.

He'd suspected for a while she had a thing for Bryce, which was why he never understood the insistence on trying to date him. Though Denise was more the warrior in that battle than Melody was. In the end, it didn't matter how Melody felt about Bryce. He was married and would never stray from Denise, even if their marriage was on the rocks.

"Hey, Bro!" Bryce slapped him on the shoulder. "What took you so long?" He glanced around the area. "Where's Eve? I figured she would've joined you."

"I tried. She doesn't like crowds. She preferred to stay in tonight."

He would've preferred that as well. Right next to her. Cuddling on the couch and pretending he was okay with the friends-only status he'd landed himself in.

"Well, so far so good. Crowd is mellow. No ruckus going on."

Griffin chuckled. "It's also only eight o'clock. We have another hour or so until the fireworks actually start."

"True. Want to take a round with me?"

By that, Bryce meant walking around the area greeting people and making small talk. Because as the mayor and chief of police, that was expected of them. Bryce and Griffin always did what was expected of them.

"I'm not singing carols this year."

Griffin had his limits. Singing Christmas carols was always a painful experience, especially since he didn't like his singing voice.

"I'm sure I can talk you into one song." Bryce's grin said he'd try like hell. Griffin wasn't having it.

Though he welcomed people, talking about this and that, his mind veered to Eve and how she was doing.

5

EVE CURLED her legs underneath her, pulling the blanket over her lap. It wasn't particularly cold in the house, especially since she had the windows open, letting in the fresh air. But it made her feel better to have it over her.

Scanning the TV didn't help steer her mind away from Griffin and Juliet and all the fun they were having. She could be having fun right now as well.

She hadn't lied, of course. Crowds were definitely not her thing.

When she was eight years old, she'd gone to the carnival with her family. It had been the best time—until she lost track of them. She could still feel the terror of searching for her parents, calling their names. Momma. Pappa. In the moment, it had never occurred to her to use their actual names. So many people. So much loudness. The panic had taken over. Instead of watching where she was going, she ran into people. In her panic-induced state, everyone bumped into her, as if shoving her around in a dizzying circle.

After what felt like hours, a police officer stopped her

and helped her find her family. They had been playing a dart game, trying to win a stuffed teddy bear. They hadn't even been aware she had wandered off and gotten lost. That had hurt more than anything.

Even then, she had been nothing. Just an object to push around and do their bidding.

Since then, it had been another reason to hate crowds. Getting lost in the sea of people.

She tossed the remote to the side, watching as it bounced on the cushion and then to the floor. It rattled across the wooden floor before stopping underneath the coffee table. She needed to buy a rug. Though the remote didn't break, it could've. A rug would've cushioned the fall better.

Sighing, she stood up and headed for the kitchen. She'd make a bowl of popcorn. The pantry door creaked as she opened it. Her eyes glossed over as she stared, thinking something didn't look right, as usual when she stared too long. She swore she put the crackers next to the popcorn, yet the box she needed sat next to the pasta. Strange.

Pushing all weird thoughts out, she grabbed a bag of microwave popcorn and shoved it into the device, hitting five minutes. She had to use the bathroom, so she rushed to the toilet, peeing as fast as she could with the door open, listening to the popcorn pop. She never actually let it pop for the full five minutes, but doing anything less never popped it correctly.

Her hands twisted under the water as she washed thoroughly, then dashed back into the kitchen right as the popcorn slowed down in its fury.

The wonderful aroma filled the kitchen even more when she opened the door, then the bag. She inhaled deeply as she poured it into a bowl. Yes, this would be a wonderful night in. Sure, she hated crowds, but fireworks weren't the best either. The loud bangs also sent her anxiety up. The pop, pop, pop one after another reminded her of things best forgotten.

Like most memories in her life. So much to forget.

She plopped back onto the couch, the bowl in her lap, realizing she needed the remote. The movie on the TV was boring. She needed something a little livelier than a slow-moving drama.

Reaching out her hand, the bowl digging into her stomach, she jerked when she heard a noise come from the kitchen. It caught her off guard so much that she lost her balance, falling off the couch. The bowl of popcorn spilled everywhere, and her head hit the edge of the coffee table.

Pain ricocheted around her forehead as she tried to sit up.

Another scrapping sound hit her senses.

She froze, waiting to hear more. But nothing.

Without making any noise besides a few crunching sounds as her hands dug into the popcorn, she raised her head to peer over the couch. She saw nothing odd. She could see the backyard, though the sun was making its descent so darkness veiled half of it.

She waited a few minutes, listening with a trained ear for any other odd sound, but nothing appeared. Her knees were killing her, holding their position for as long as she was. With an aching slowness, she stood up, putting a hand to her head that still echoed with pain. She felt no deep gash, but the ache told her she'd knocked herself good.

Her steps were quiet as she made her way to the kitchen for the broom. The tiny closet where she kept the cleaning supplies creaked as the pantry had. Before going back to the living room to clean up her mess, she flipped the outside light on and stared into the backyard. Still, nothing appeared out of place.

She made another cursory glance at everything. Her heart stilled when she eyed the small planter sitting on the edge of the concrete patio. It was lying on its side.

Someone had knocked it over. Or something, like an animal.

Yes, an animal.

She gripped the broom handle harder. But what kind of animal? The edge of the woods was a distance away, so it made it difficult to see if anything was hiding amongst the trees and bushes. She saw nothing, staring long and hard. Oh, to have a fenced-in backyard like Griffin had. Too bad she was only renting, otherwise she would've found the money somewhere to have a fence put up around her yard to feel more secure.

Double checking the lock on the sliding door, she found it secure. That should've made her feel better. It only increased the fear slithering up and down her spine.

Had he found her?

Was he outside?

There weren't many places to hide in the yard itself, especially with the light glowing in the backyard. But all anyone needed to do was wait along the edge of the tree line, in the darkness, waiting to spring to action. Or on the side of the house.

Well, she wasn't sticking around to find out who it was. She gripped the broom in one hand, while snatching her purse in the other, then slipped on a pair of sandals. Her fingers fumbled with her keys as she locked her front door, then she dashed to her car, shoving the broom in the front seat.

What was she doing?

Where should she go?

Flee town? But to where?

And why? It could've been an animal that knocked over the pot.

Her hands gripped the wheel, her heart pounding. When she saw the shadow emerge from the side of the house, she whipped the car in reverse and flew out of the driveway.

Definitely not an animal that had made the noises.

She drove with no destination in mind. Last time she had two days to plan her escape. This was spur of the moment and she had no idea where to run to, and with nothing but her purse.

When she saw all the cars lined up on the side of the road, the parking lot so full near the lake, she knew exactly where to go.

To Griffin.

He'd help her. He'd protect her as it was his duty.

Except he didn't know her problems. That she'd broken the law. As a man who believed wholeheartedly in right and wrong, he might not forgive her for her offenses, no matter the reason.

No. She couldn't stop. She had to keep driving until a plan formed in her mind. She had no idea how he had found her, but he had. She wasn't safe here any longer.

Her foot pushed harder on the gas pedal until she had no choice but to slam on the brakes when Duke stepped into her path and put his hand out.

He approached her vehicle, forcing her to roll down the window and produce a smile that she knew looked lopsided.

"Hey, Eve. The parking lot is full. Sorry. Why don't you pull over behind my vehicle? You won't be blocked in." He pointed to his patrol car near the entrance to the lake. There was enough space for her tiny car to fit behind his and not block the road or the entrance.

"Eve?" His brows furrowed as he leaned closer to the window. "You okay?"

Her smile brightened, even as her insides coiled with fright. "Yes, of course. Thank you, Officer Fisk."

"It's Duke. You know that." Then he winked and gestured for her to park.

She had no choice. If she raced out of town now, he might follow. She couldn't allow that. He'd arrest her for fleeing. He'd take her prints. The jig would be up. Of course, fleeing for what? She was making this more than what it should be. All she had to do was remain calm and in control.

Her hands shook as she parked the car, grabbed her purse, and exited the vehicle. She threw out another fake smile, waving to Duke.

Her anxiety ratcheted up another notch as she wove through the large crowd searching for Griffin or Juliet. Now that she was here, she had to find one of them.

She found Bryce first.

"Hey, I thought you weren't coming."

Her hands twisted to and fro, before she realized what she was doing, forcing herself to relax. "I changed my mind. Not much on TV."

Bryce grinned his easygoing smile that always made her smile in return. She didn't have as many interactions with him as she did with Griffin and Juliet, but she felt safe in his presence. He was always kind to her, joking as he did with Juliet. They were all such nice people.

Though she returned a smile, it felt so forced she swore her face was going to break in half.

"Come on. The fireworks are going to start soon. Griffin and Juliet are over here."

She followed on his tail, tossing her purse over her neck so it draped across her chest.

The terror that had been running through her veins since the moment she heard the noise lessened a fraction when she made eye contact with Griffin.

His genuine smile eased her nerves even more when he stood up as she got closer.

Juliet noticed her as well. "Girl, you came! You're just in time. They're going to start any minute."

Her lips twisted into a grin, meeting Juliet's gaze, then she swiveled back to Griffin. Bryce took a seat next to his wife, Denise. A woman she didn't speak to much, Melody, sat next to her. She looked at her but didn't acknowledge her in any way.

Then Griffin held out his hand.

She took it, even knowing she couldn't hide the trembles coating her body. The second she made contact with him, she knew everything would be okay. He'd keep her safe.

GRIFFIN KNEW something was wrong but didn't want to put her on the spot in front of everyone. He didn't think it had anything to do with the large crowd. The fear in her eyes was palpable. The quaking in her hand wasn't hard to miss.

He tightened his grip, pulling her gently to sit down next to him. Despite all the times he reminded himself it was a bad idea to forget they were only friends, he put his arm around her, pulling her into his body.

She melted into his embrace, sighing. Her head rested against his chest, and he couldn't help but kiss the top of her head. She stiffened at the contact. He braced himself for her to shove him away. She didn't move. If anything, she leaned even closer.

He wanted to ask what was wrong, what had happened, but he couldn't find the words. Conversations darted around them. Juliet's merry laughter. Melody's obnoxious laugh. Kids squealing in delight. Men hooting and hollering. So much commotion going on and he was frozen.

Eve wore the same clothes he had seen her in before leaving. Not that she couldn't come out in public dressed so casually, but it was abnormal for her. He'd never seen her leave the house in sweatpants.

The first bang in the sky came out of nowhere. Eve flinched, turning her head even more into his chest. She wasn't even looking up at the sky.

Why had she come then?

What had frightened her?

Firework after firework exploded, lighting up the sky.

Chatter wove around them, but more deluded as the bangs coating the air took residence over anything else.

He grasped her more firmly, placing another kiss on her head. This time she didn't flinch. Despite the colors painting the sky, his eyes were on her. Question after question pelted his mind and he didn't know where to start. He needed to know why she'd come. Why she appeared so scared.

"I got you," he whispered finally, still unsure of the right thing to say.

Her arms, which had been tucked to her stomach, wove around his body. Then her fingers gripped his shirt.

The fireworks were over before he knew it. No questions had left his lips. He peered over her head, making contact with Juliet, who frowned. His eyes belayed the unasked question. He had no idea what happened. She nodded, packing up her belongings along with the things he had brought. Even Bryce, Denise, and Melody said nothing to them as they also packed up.

The crowd dispersed, and Griffin sat on the blanket holding Eve. She didn't lift her head once.

He had no idea how much time had passed before they were the only ones left in the park. Quiet surrounded them for the first time that night.

He lowered his lips to press another kiss to the top of her hair when her head lifted. His lips landed on her nose instead.

She shivered at the touch, her hands grasping his shirt even more, to the point he felt her nails scrape his skin.

Though it was dark out, the park had a few streetlamps lighting the area. With her eyes finally meeting his, he could see a red mark on her forehead.

He lifted his hand, brushing her hair and her skin lightly across the mark.

"What happened?"

"I..." She let out a tiny breath, closing her eyes.

This time his lips caressed the mark, making her shiver once again.

"Talk to me, Eve. What happened tonight? You didn't look at the fireworks once, so I know you didn't come here for that."

Her eyes opened.

His fingers dusted across the mark. "What's this from? You hurt yourself."

"I fell off the couch. Hit my head on the coffee table."

He waited, knowing there was more to the story. Waiting for the reason *why* she fell off the couch.

"I thought someone was in the backyard. I heard a few noises. It startled me. My planter was knocked over."

His fingers dug into her skin, his hold on her strengthening. She trembled but didn't move away, so he knew it wasn't from fear he was harming her.

"You should've called me. I would've come over right away. Did you see someone?"

A quick shake of her head answered him, though her eyes betrayed her as if she lied to him. Why lie about it?

"I'll drive you home. I'll take a look around."

She nodded, lifting her head some more. The position put her in better alignment with his. A quick dip and he could kiss her. Taste her sweet lips.

Her eyes glistened with desire as if she wanted the same thing. Then she tore her gaze away, making him curse inside for losing his chance.

He helped her stand, then picked up the blanket, rolling it into a mess, not bothering to fold it. She giggled, a beautiful sound to his ears, then took the blanket from him, folding it properly.

He decided to test the waters between them. He always kept his distance, his hands away from her. Touching wouldn't lead to anything innocent. But having her in his arms, holding her so close, his body craved more. His heart needed more.

He scooped her hand into his, waiting for her to pull away. His heart skipped a beat when her fingers slid between his, interlocking their grip even further.

They headed for his vehicle, holding hands.

She hopped into the passenger seat, the blanket resting on her lap. When he came to the road, he saw her car parked.

"I can drive home, Grif. I'm opening the cafe tomorrow. I need it."

"I'll drive you to the cafe and I'll make sure you get your car before your shift ends."

Her brows puckered, and he waited for her to argue. When she said nothing, he turned right, heading home.

The drive wasn't long. She handed over her keys, so he could take a look around her house. She remained in his vehicle while he did so. He saw the popcorn scattered around the couch and on the floor. Obviously, she fell off with the bowl in her lap. Something had definitely frightened her. The house was empty, and besides the popcorn mess, it looked the way it should. Nobody was in the backyard, and the lock was secure on the sliding glass door. The planter she said had been turned over was sitting upright. No dirt lingered around the area indicating it had been toppled. Someone fixed it.

Hmm. That was odd.

As soon as he stepped outside, she hopped out of the vehicle.

"Well?"

He smiled, hoping to ease the fear in her eyes. "I didn't see anything odd. Just the mess in the living room. The planter isn't on its side."

"What?" She shook her head, walking past him inside the house. "I saw it. It was knocked over."

She did the same thing he had. Inspected around the ground, looking for evidence it had tipped over. When she stepped back into the kitchen, she slammed the sliding door closed.

"I swear it was on its side. I heard noises. I saw a shadow figure coming from the side of the house when I backed out of the driveway."

Finally! She confessed she saw someone. Well, the shadow of someone. Why not tell him right away? Well, it didn't matter. Someone was here and that person frightened her.

He walked to the sliding door and flipped the lock so neither of them forgot to do so. Then he stopped in front of her, aching to touch her again. Anything. Even a brush of her cheek.

"I believe you."

Her wounded eyes looked up at him. "You do?"

"Why wouldn't I?"

The hesitation in her gaze told him she'd been doubted by someone in her past.

"Thank you, Grif."

He nodded, fisting his hands to stop himself from reaching out to her. He sensed he'd already pressed his luck. She'd allowed more touching than he normally did. "I'll clean up the popcorn mess. Where's your broom?"

A sweet smile hit her lips. "In the front seat of my car. I kind of ran out of the house with it."

"I'll go grab mine."

Then he walked away before he did something stupid— like kiss her breathless.

6

JULIET WALKED into the back area, her lips spreading wide. "This smell is divine."

Eve chuckled, continuing the rolling of the dough. From there she'd cut the dough into triangles and then roll each one up into croissants.

After spending a lot longer than she should've on the couch with Griffin last night, she should've been bone tired. Instead, she felt on top of the world. His mere presence had calmed her like nothing ever had before.

The longer she thought about it, the more she decided her eyes had to have been playing tricks on her. Maybe someone had been roaming around the house, but not a speck of dirt littered the ground. If the planter had fallen over and someone picked it up, they had cleaned it spectacularly to hide the evidence.

Or maybe her mind had imagined the planter on its side. She'd been jumping at every shadow since she arrived, so it only made sense she conjured something that didn't happen.

Despite the tenderness he had bestowed upon her

during the fireworks, he remained a gentleman the rest of the evening. He sat on one side of the couch while she sat on the other. Being a loveseat, it didn't offer a lot of room, but no body parts touched. For some reason, that disappointed her. Starting a relationship so soon, and one filled with lies, wouldn't be wise. Yet, she wanted to. She wanted more from Griffin, and that was a problem.

She'd been ready to flee last night, and it still sounded like a good idea. She wasn't safe in this town any longer. Because she was losing her heart to a kind, decent man. Lying to him was getting harder and harder to do.

Juliet kept on her merry chatter she loved doing. Chip nodded in usual fashion, and Eve participated when she had to. The only odd thing about the day was Juliet not asking about last night. About why she showed up at the park. Did that mean Griffin had told her? She wasn't sure how she felt about that. If she wanted Juliet—or anyone else—to know what happened, it should be her decision, no one else's.

Her shift ended at two, and Griffin delivered her car as promised. He'd stopped in around eleven for lunch, returning her keys and letting her know it was parked in back. He didn't say anything about last night and neither did she. What was there to say? Nothing had happened between them. Still platonic as usual.

He confirmed they were on for grilling steaks tonight. While she wanted to bow out somehow, she nodded, though she still had an escape to plan once again.

She had her key in the lock of her car when Juliet called out to her.

"Everything okay, Eve? I told myself not to pry, but I wanted to make sure."

"Of course."

Juliet walked closer. "You came last night, but everything didn't seem okay. Griffin hasn't told me anything, and I'm worried. You looked...frightened last night."

She still was. Perhaps her mind had been playing tricks on her. Or maybe she had seen exactly what she thought. Then that meant he found her.

Honestly, would she ever be safe? Always looking over her shoulder. Always ready to flee at a moment's notice. Always keeping people at a distance because it wasn't wise to let them get too close.

Look at what happened letting Griffin penetrate her defenses. She let her guard down. She let herself feel safe when she was anything but.

"Eve? You can tell me anything. You can trust me." Juliet stepped even closer, so close she could reach out and touch her. "You can trust Griffin."

Eve sighed, her heart sinking at the realization hitting her. "I can't trust anyone, Juliet. I wish I could."

Then she opened her car door, making Juliet move to the side. She pulled out of the lot, eyeing Juliet in her rearview mirror, noting the phone to her ear.

She shouldn't have been so honest. Now she had no choice. No time to plan. She had to leave now. Speeding wasn't an option as one of the officers was always patrolling the streets. She felt as if she always passed one driving anywhere she went in town, no matter the day or time.

Her legs felt like Jell-O as she exited her car and rushed to her door. She stood for a moment, wondering what to pack. There was no time to grab a lot. Juliet had called someone. That someone had to have been Griffin. Would he come over immediately? Wait to talk to her tonight? She couldn't risk him coming right now.

Grabbing her duffle bag from the closet, the same one

she fled with the first time, she tossed as many clothes as she could in there. Toiletries went in next. She'd take her pillow as well, and one blanket. If she had to sleep in her car, then she'd at least have some comfort.

Food. She'd need some to hold her over until she had a decent plan. Whatever that plan was, she had no idea. Maybe something would come to her on the drive out of town.

She turned from her bed, stopping in her tracks. Griffin stood in the doorway, blocking her exit. His eyes glided to the bag on the bed, filled to the brim. Then his gaze met hers.

"You left your front door open."

Had she? She didn't remember. All she recollected was running out of the car and standing in the foyer for a moment, wondering what to pack.

"Silly me. Thank you for letting me know."

His eyes darted to the bag again. "Going somewhere?"

She swallowed, feeling the sweat build up in her armpits. She hated constantly lying to him. But she had no choice.

"I need some non-Christmas stuff. You know how hard it is to buy anything like that here. I thought I'd take an overnight bag."

"Where are you going?" His stare was intense, as if he looked hard enough he'd see all her secrets.

"Out of town for a few days."

His brows burrowed even lower than before. "And what about steaks tonight? Are you canceling plans with me? Or are you leaving tomorrow? I didn't realize you asked Juliet for some time off."

She hadn't. This was all a spur-of-the-moment thing. If Juliet had left her alone and not said anything about last night, she wouldn't be running. At least, not yet. She would've had dinner with Griffin. She would've soaked up a bit more of his kindness, his sweet smiles and wonderful laugh. Perhaps even a touch or two.

"Yes, I do have to cancel plans tonight. I need—"

"You need to stop lying to me," he cut her off with a harsh growl.

The anger in his tone had her taking a step back, her shoulders cringing inward, shielding herself from a potential blow.

GRIFFIN CURSED himself for frightening her—again. He had to keep his cool, his anger in check. It wasn't her fault she was terrified. That she thought she had to leave. He kept his distance a little too much. He took more time than he should've trying to gain her trust. He realized that now.

Getting that phone call from Juliet that Eve would run sent his heart into a tailspin. She couldn't leave. Not like this. Not if she was in danger.

He softened his expression, quieting his tone of voice.

"I'm not going to hurt you, Eve. I'm not going to stop you from leaving either. But," he said, taking one tiny step into the room, "I am going to try to convince you to trust me. To tell me what has you so frightened. Why'd you tell Juliet you can't trust anyone? If you need help, I'm here for that. You have to know that. So is Juliet. Bryce as well."

Her body seemed to relax a fraction.

"Did someone hurt you? Are you running from someone?"

She tensed once again.

Damn it! He was screwing this up left and right.

How did he show her she could trust him? After the last two months, she should know he'd do anything for her.

He stepped farther into the room but to the side of the doorway. Enough space for her to leave without him getting in the way.

He gestured at the exit. "See, you can leave. Go on your mini trip. I'll be here waiting for you to get back. We'll have steaks then."

Just like the time she wanted to leave without eating his lasagna, he was giving her a way out. Making sure she knew she wasn't trapped. She held the power and control of the situation.

She glanced at him, then the doorway. He could see the indecision written on her face. His stomach twisted in pain when she grabbed her bag and slung it over her shoulder. He felt like someone shoved a knife in his gut when she walked past him without a word.

She was truly going to leave without telling him why.

He didn't move, not wanting to scare her any further. He heard rustling in the kitchen as if she were grabbing as much food as she could for the road. She'd need it if she was going on the run again.

He clenched his fists, then unclenched them, telling himself not to move an inch. He couldn't stop her. It wasn't his place. But damn it, he wanted to. He wanted to beg her to trust him, to know that whatever problems she had he'd fix them. Or die trying.

He closed his eyes, his heart breaking in two when he heard the front door close. She was officially gone. He knew he'd never see her again.

"I shouldn't have said I'd make potato salad. It should marinate in the sauce to get a good flavor for at least a day. I didn't have time to make it last night. Honestly, I forgot to make it."

His eyes flew open. Eve stood in the doorway. No bag on her shoulder. No purse in her hand. No food by her side. Just her and the fright in her eyes.

"I have fixings for a salad. We can have that instead." His heart pounded at the realization she hadn't left.

But she still could. He felt like he was right back on that shaky ground and one wrong move would send him tumbling to his death.

She took a step into the room. "You would've let me leave."

"I still will. Not that I want you to."

Her gaze hit the floor. "I'm scared, Grif."

He approached her slowly and lifted her chin with his hand. She didn't back away. "I know. I sense it all the time. I was trying to take this slow. Let you tell me in your own time what's wrong. I'm having a hard time doing that now."

"How did you know?"

His hand lowered to his side. "As Juliet said, classic signs. She would know as her ex-husband is currently sitting in prison for beating her."

Eve flinched, her eyes widening in surprise.

"She didn't tell me or Bryce for a long time. I couldn't be mad at her because I was more mad at myself for not seeing it. But as soon as I knew, I made sure that bastard never hurt her again. I will do the same for you."

"I can't let you do that."

He frowned. "Why the hell not?"

She bit her bottom lip. "You'll hate me for some of the things I had to do. For...for some of the lies I had to tell. I think it's best I leave. For everyone."

"Why don't you tell me those things and I make my own decision on how I feel about it."

Because Griffin didn't think he'd hate her for any reason, no matter what lies she might've told.

"I can't."

"No, Eve, you won't. There's a difference."

"See, you are mad at me. You do hate me."

He groaned in frustration, shaking his head. This woman could drive him insane with the least provocation. She had no idea the ache she filled him with every day. Every night.

He framed her face and pressed his lips to hers before he could change his mind and she could protest. He waited a moment for her to push him away and break the touch, and when she didn't, he deepened the pressure.

She leaned into him, opening her mouth. He didn't delay in the small victory, in the acceptance she bestowed upon him.

His tongue dipped in, coaxing her to play, to enjoy the kiss with everything she had. Her low moan was all he needed to know that she wanted this. Wanted him.

His hands moved from her cheeks to her backside, crushing her to his chest. Her hands wound around him, holding on. The way she clung to him, her hands gripping the back of his shirt ignited the fire even more inside of him. The kiss turned hotter, his tongue now dueling instead of playing. She matched him twist for twist of the lips.

His fingers slid down her back, cupping her ass. Another moan slipped from her lips, encouraging him to keep going. He picked her up, groaning in approval when her legs attached around his waist. He walked until his legs hit the mattress. Then he lowered her to the bed, pinning her down but not crushing her.

The kiss slowed, then ended, his lips trailing across her chin to her neck where he took tiny nibbles.

He was hard as a rock and his cock nestled perfectly in the right place. The only problem was the clothes acting as a barrier and the things left unsaid. They should talk more before anything else happened.

He lifted his head, meeting her dazed eyes. "Does that feel like a man who hates you? Or is mad at you? The only thing I feel is torture of not having you. Of wanting you day after day knowing I need to take it slow. I know you've lied to me. I know you have secrets you're not ready to share. And I'm telling you right now that I will wait for you to confess them in your own time."

"That scares me too, Grif. How much I want you in return."

He brushed a lock of hair away from her cheek. "Promise me one thing, Eve. Only one thing."

He waited for her to acknowledge his plea. She gave a tight nod.

"You'll tell me you're leaving. Don't run from me. I need to know if you want to leave."

She inhaled a deep breath and let it out in slow increments. "I promise."

"How about those steaks then?"

"I'll make the salad."

7

Juliet tossed a bean bag to her, nodding in approval. "Okay, you're on my team. Let's beat their asses."

Eve giggled at Juliet's competitiveness. A week had passed since her mini panic attack. Things had gone back to normal as if it never happened. Griffin didn't pressure her to spill her secrets. Juliet made no comment on her rushing away from her.

The only difference was Griffin wasn't afraid to show affection anymore. Like now. He pressed a light kiss to her lips before winking and taking the other side of the corn-hole. Bryce stood on the other side of the yard with Juliet next to him. They were going to play a game and Juliet thought they were going to win. Ha! She might've caught the bean bag, but she had terrible aim.

But she'd have fun regardless.

The four played as if they had no cares in the world. Bryce pretended as if his marriage wasn't heading for divorce. Eve had arrived with Griffin at Bryce's house. Shortly after getting there, they witnessed Denise shouting nasty things at Bryce before peeling out of the driveway. She had let Griffin have a word alone with Bryce, which hadn't lasted long. He didn't want to talk about it. She understood that.

She didn't want to talk about her issues either.

Every time she thought she found the courage, the words got stuck in her throat. She'd come to the conclusion she had imagined the planter on its side and the shadowy figure coming from the side of the house. Considering nothing else odd had happened in the past week, she had to have imagined it.

Griffin didn't pressure her. He didn't even bring the subject up. That made it harder for her to confess. Though she couldn't blame him for her inability to speak. It was her fault. Her weakness.

The men won the first round.

They won the second round too.

When Juliet suggested a third game, Eve bowed out.

"A tiny break. My arm is starting to hurt."

Which was a lie. She hated to lose. Hated looking like a loser.

"Fine," Juliet grumbled, though wore a smile.

She grabbed a pop from the cooler and jumped a little when she stood, turning around. Griffin stood in front of her. He did that so often. Appearing out of nowhere and making her jump.

He brushed her cheek before kissing her. Briefly, as they had an audience, but enough to ignite her senses, wanting more.

"You know you don't have to..." He paused as if looking for the right words. "Stretch the truth."

"I don't know what you mean."

His fingers caressed her throwing arm. "I've come to learn your smiles. I know when you're telling a lie. It's okay to want to take a break from the game. Saying your arm hurts isn't necessary."

In her past life, it had been. Lying had been a mechanism to survive. Feigning headaches to bow out of invites so they wouldn't see the bruises. Pretending she was dining with one friend when another asked her for lunch only to stay at home because it hurt to move. Lying had been a way of life to hide the ugly parts she couldn't let anyone see. Because sometimes he didn't hit her where it could easily be covered up. He never cared how he treated her.

His fingers slid back up her arm, eliciting a delightful shiver from her. She smiled at the contact.

"So if I say...I like it when you touch me like that, you know I'm not lying."

His lips brimmed with pleasure, his fingers taking the same path as before. Up then down. "Yes, I know you're not lying about that. I can see it in your eyes. I can sense it in your touch. The shivers of delight compared to ones of fear." His smile fell. "I need you to know that none of us are going to get mad if you tell us something. That you're tired and just want to quit. That you want to leave because you've had enough. It's okay to be honest with us. We will understand."

"I suck at cornhole. My aim is terrible. I hate losing."

She knew she sounded whiny, but he said to be honest, so she was going to try it out.

"My Eve has a competitive streak in her. Hating to lose. How about I teach you some moves." He leaned closer. "Or, better yet, you be on my team."

"No, if I win, I want it to be with Juliet. Men vs women."

His lips moved closer. "But I like you on my team. I like you by my side."

"I am by your side."

"Are you?"

She knew the question was deeper than just him suggesting she stood by him playing the game. Before she could give any kind of answer, his lips connected with hers. Longer and more intense than any other one before.

A low moan filtered between them, causing him to wrap his arms around her to pull her closer. That elicited another pleasured moan from her lips.

"Get a room, you two! Let's play some cards," Juliet shouted from the other end of the yard.

Griffin chuckled against her lips, then pulled away, grabbing her hand. "How are you at cards?"

She felt the lie rising to the surface but shoved it down. "About as good as I am at cornhole."

His deep laughter filled her heart with joy. "And I guess you still want to be on Juliet's team."

"Of course. I will eventually win against you."

He smiled but didn't respond.

They all took a seat around the table on the deck. Bryce shuffled the deck of cards first. The games they started to play didn't require teams. Five card draw. Texas Hold'em. Poker games she had to learn every time they introduced a new one. But in the end, it didn't matter she lost every hand; she had fun.

Five hours later, after Bryce grilled hamburgers, they left. Griffin pulled into his driveway, putting the vehicle in park. He looked at his house then glanced at hers before meeting her gaze.

"Want to come in and watch a movie or something?"

This was the first time since arriving in town and hanging out with Griffin that they'd spent the entire day together. Every other time had always been after work or on their day off but only for a few hours. He didn't want the time to end and neither did she.

"Or something. Sure."

His eyes glittered with passion at her suggestive meaning. Though after the words came out, the worry slipped in. Was she ready for that level? To sleep with him and put her heart even further in his hands?

It would only make it harder to leave. When she eventually had to. Because even though it'd been a decent week, she had running on her mind all the time.

He must've sensed where her thoughts slithered to because he slid his hand into hers.

"I'll make popcorn if you want some."

He had such an easy way of turning the situation from panic-inducing to an even keel.

"I'd like that. I want to run home and change." She looked down at her shirt where ketchup had spilled.

"I don't mind a little ketchup."

She giggled. "Well, I do."

He lifted their hands, kissing the back of hers before letting her go. "I'll make some Kool-Aid to go with the popcorn."

"Sounds wonderful."

And it did. Everything Griffin always did was spectacular. He made her feel so safe and secure all the time.

He jaunted up his sidewalk while she dashed across her yard. Her house felt stuffy the moment she opened the door. Weird. The air-conditioner must not be working. She'd turned it on a few days ago when the temps rose a little higher than she liked. Fresh air was nice, but the humidity wasn't always great.

She froze in her bedroom when she saw the curtains to the side and the window open. They hadn't been like that when she left. She would've remembered opening the window. Yes, the curtains she'd tossed to the side to let in the sunlight. And perhaps give Griffin a view or two of her changing from her PJs to her clothes. It had been naughty of her this morning when she saw him rummaging in his kitchen, and she found herself doing it anyway. Whether he watched her undress she wasn't sure. He didn't comment on it when they left for Bryce's.

But she had never opened the window.

She backed out of the room, listening for anything out of place. She heard nothing but her heavy, uncontrolled breathing. A glance at the thermostat in the hallway showed it off. She never turned it off.

Had she?

Why was she constantly questioning herself? Not remembering doing something when she had obviously done it. If not her, then someone was breaking into her house way too much.

She stalked to the sliding door, double-checking it was locked. It didn't budge. How would they have gotten in? The front door had been locked as had the sliding door. Though the window was open now, she had closed and locked it. Right? She honestly didn't remember opening it.

Maybe she was losing her mind and she had turned off the thermostat and opened her window. A quick run-through of her house showed nothing else out of place.

She walked back over to Griffin's, stepping inside without knocking. He knew she was coming over so why bother?

He set the popcorn bowl on the coffee table, looking at her, his brows puckering as he stared at her shirt.

"I thought you went to change."

She followed his gaze, realizing in her panic she never switched shirts.

"Eve?" He rounded the table with quick strides, cupping her cheek gently yet firmly. "What's wrong?"

She lifted her eyes to his, the fear slithering up and down her spine.

"I think I'm losing my mind."

GRIFFIN STARED at the open window.

"I remember opening the curtains and not closing them, but I don't remember opening the window."

He nodded. "Yeah, I don't think you closed the curtains."

His cheeks flamed as the memory assaulted him. The way she removed her shirt, tossing it on the ground. Her pert breasts on display, his hands aching to touch and caress until she uttered the low moans she enjoyed when he kissed her.

His eyes met hers. The sweet grin on her face said she knew that he'd seen her this morning.

"You were watching this morning?"

He matched her grin. "You never open your curtains. I thought it was an invitation to watch."

This time her cheeks burned a bright red, her eyes casting to the floor. "Did you like what you saw?"

"Eve, there isn't anything I don't like about you."

Her eyes popped up to his. They stared at each other for a moment. Even her lies weren't enough to turn him away, though it got harder each day to hold his patience in. When would she trust him? How much more did he need to display that he'd do everything in his power to keep her safe?

He tossed a hand toward the window. "If you think

someone was in here, that you didn't open the window, I can dust for prints."

Her eyes widened. "Umm..."

"If someone broke in, I want them to pay for their crimes. Don't you?"

She shivered, wrapping her arms around her body. The instinctive move she always did when she was shielding herself from harm. He'd never hurt her. Why couldn't she understand that?

"It will be quick and I'll clean up after. I would need a set of your prints to rule out any prints that might be yours."

At that statement, she took a step back as if ready to run.

"No, that's okay. I opened it and forgot." She snapped her fingers. "Yep, I'm pretty sure I did."

"Is there something you're afraid I'll find if I run your prints?" He held up his hand before she could speak. "If you can't answer without lying don't say anything at all."

She swallowed and didn't respond, which was answer enough. Yes, she was afraid he'd see something he wouldn't like. Damn it! He needed her to spill her secrets before he went crazy.

"Okay, if you think you opened it, we'll leave it at that. How about that movie?"

Continuing to ignore the huge elephant in the room wasn't going to help them move forward as a couple. And damn it, they were a couple. He wouldn't accept anything less. But he swore to her he'd take this at her pace, and he wasn't going to go back on his word.

"Let me close the window and change my shirt. I'll be right over."

He conceded knowing nothing he said would change her mind.

Four days later, he sat in his office staring into space,

contemplating something he knew would send their relationship in the wrong direction.

"Knock, knock."

He looked over to his doorway to see Juliet standing there. She stepped in, closed the door, then set a bag on his desk.

"You called in the order and then never picked it up. Eve was worried something bad happened to you. I assured her you simply forgot, which seems to be the truth." Juliet slumped in the chair, staring quizzically at him. "The question is why you forgot."

"I'm not sure how much longer I can be patient with Eve. I know she's lied to me. To all of us. I know she's running from someone. I know that someone hurt her. I've done everything to make her feel safe and relaxed and that she can trust me, and still nothing. She won't talk about any of it."

Juliet was quiet for the longest time. Griffin chose to remain silent as well. He needed someone else's opinion on the matter and Juliet seemed like the best candidate for it. He only needed to be patient. Something he was seriously losing by the minute.

"It's not easy to talk about some things, Grif. You might have locked Gerald up because he beat me badly that night, but there are things I'll never tell you because they're too hard to talk about."

And Griffin hated knowing that.

To think that bastard hurt his sister so badly she couldn't even tell her brothers what it was.

"Eve thinks someone was in her house."

Juliet sat up straighter.

That got her attention as he knew it would. It also confirmed Eve didn't tell Juliet everything, despite sharing most things with him. That warmed his heart to know she at least trusted him in some sense.

"Why does she think that?"

"There was a window open. She doesn't remember opening it. Something little, I know." Griffin shrugged. "But it frightened her. So I suggested dusting for prints. Easy enough to see if someone was inside that shouldn't have been."

Juliet nodded as if she agreed.

"The thought I'd take her prints to match hers on the window to rule those prints out scared her more than the thought someone had opened it."

Juliet slumped back in her chair.

"Which makes me believe Eve Johnson isn't her real name. I ran the name. It's such a common name, way too many results popped up. It would take me days to run through them all."

"You're treading dangerous waters here, Grif. If she knew you did that..."

He slammed his hand on the desk. "I want to protect her! How can I do that without all the answers?" His eyes glided to the coffee cup sitting near the edge of his desk. Juliet's eyes followed his.

"Are you asking if you should dig deeper without her permission?"

"I'm asking how do I take care of the woman I'm falling in love with."

Juliet leaned forward, reaching out her hands as if to offer comfort and like he'd take it. He didn't want that from her. He wanted to hear what he knew he shouldn't do.

"Grif..." She shook her head. "If you don't want your heart broken even more, you need to do what you need to do. Bottom line, your feelings matter too. But I'm worried about her like you are." Her eyes slid to the coffee cup. "Why'd you look at that?"

"We strolled around the block this morning enjoying a cup of coffee. She forgot a hair tie at home, and I said I had a spare in my office. She left her cup here."

Juliet snorted. "Why do you have a spare hair tie in your office?"

Griffin rolled his eyes. "Because I have a sister who leaves shit everywhere she goes."

She pondered that for a moment before giggling and nodding in agreement.

"If I pull her prints from that cup, I might find something I don't like."

"There's no might about it, Grif. We both know you will." She stood up, pointing to the cup. "Let me know when you have the results. I'll be there with you when you talk to her about it."

Having his sister's approval didn't lessen the rapid beat of his heart.

He pulled prints from the cup and ran them.

He had been right.

He didn't like the results.

8

THE WEEK ROLLED BY FAST, bringing Saturday around once again. Instead of hanging out grilling and playing games at Bryce's house, Griffin decided to host. Eve put the potato salad she made yesterday in the fridge, then joined Juliet outside. Bryce had yet to arrive.

She took a seat next to Juliet, who'd been quiet the last three days. Not her usual bubbly self. Eve had asked her once if everything was okay, and while Juliet had confirmed it was, Eve sensed she had lied. She'd know, since she did it so often herself.

"When's Bryce getting here? He's normally so punctual."

Juliet shook her head as if shaking off the aftereffects of daydreaming. "Oh, I didn't call him. I should've."

Odd. Eve assumed this would be a repeat of last weekend. Griffin hadn't ventured outside yet. She didn't know where he was. Juliet had let her in, then walked outside in the backyard without chatting. While she'd seen Griffin in the cafe for lunch, she hadn't spent any time with him after work like she normally did.

Something was very wrong.

"Where's Griffin?"

Juliet looked at her as if confused by the question. Something was going on and she didn't like it.

Eve stood up. Juliet followed suit.

Both of them turned to the sound of the sliding door opening. Griffin stepped out holding a manila folder.

Tension rolled around her shoulders. Anxiety coursed through her veins. The need to run slammed into her chest.

"Why don't we all sit, Eve?" Juliet smiled, though Eve heard the tension in her voice.

"What's going on here?"

"I think we should—"

"No!" Eve shouted, cutting off Griffin. "Tell me what's going on here. What's in the folder?"

They stared at each other, waiting for the other to start.

Griffin finally answered by pulling out a piece of paper and laying it on the table. Her driver's license photo from Florida stared back at her.

Evelyn Carrington.

The truth was out.

"Evelyn—"

She recoiled at the sound of her full name on Griffin's lips, stumbling back, nearly tumbling to the ground when she tripped on her feet.

"Please don't call me that," she whispered, unable to look either of them in the eye.

She didn't dare look around the yard, but she tried to recall if Griffin had a lock on the gate in the backyard. How easily could she get away? He probably didn't because he felt safe. Unlike her who would've needed that extra barrier to keep people out.

"Look, Eve, I know this comes as a shock, but we did this

out of love," Juliet insisted in that same calm voice as before, but the tension still lingered.

Love? No, this was an ambush. He said she could confess in her own time. He lied.

And he signed her death warrant.

He had no idea the wrath he dropped on her head.

"When did you do this? How did you do this?" Her head snapped up, glaring.

He flinched at her hard stare. "I pulled prints from the coffee cup you left in my office three days ago. I had to know why you didn't want me to run your prints."

Three days ago.

No wonder Griffin had kept his distance the last few days. Because he despised her now. Wanted nothing to do with her. Waiting to arrest her.

Oh God.

The even worse part was *he* could already be here. Hiding. Waiting. Plotting her demise.

Griffin pulled another sheet of paper out, laying it on top of the other one. This one also had her picture on it. This time with the large word MISSING written underneath.

Ha! She wasn't missing. She chose to hide.

"You were reported missing over two months ago. I haven't done anything about it, and I need to know how to handle this."

She frowned at his choice of words.

"What?"

He set the folder down, covering the picture. Then he took a few steps her way. He stopped when he saw her retreat for every step he took.

"You're living under a fake name. You're working under a fake name. That's just one reason I could arrest you."

"Grif!" Juliet huffed.

Eve prepared her stance to run. She had to hope she could outrun him.

"I need you to talk to me. Tell me who you're running from."

No. She couldn't now. No matter what she said, he'd only see the laws she broke. This was why she never wanted to confess anything in the first place. He was a lawman first, man second.

She turned and made a run for it. The fence gate was in her reach with no lock hindering her path. Strong arms grabbed her from behind, pulling her against his chest. She struggled, kicking and hitting, hating that she might hurt him in the process, yet it didn't stop her from trying to escape. She never could from *him*, so she didn't know why she thought it'd work with Griffin.

Their struggles brought them tumbling to the ground. Griffin got the upper hand, pinning her body and shoving her hands above her head. They both were breathing heavily, staring at each other.

"The last three days were the hardest days of my life, trying to stay away from you so I didn't explode."

"So you wouldn't hurt me?" she whispered, tugging on her hands so he'd let her go. Telling him he was hurting her, even though he really wasn't. His grip was tight but gentle.

He leaned closer. "I would never hurt you."

Then his lips caressed hers. So softly, it's as if she imagined it.

"I'm so filled with rage right now I can barely contain it." He let her hands go, brushing hair away from her cheek. "Not at you. I'm not mad at you. I'm angry at the fact you had to run away to save yourself. I'm angry that you thought you couldn't trust me with this information. I'm angry that my job dictates I respond to what I found and I can't seem to do it. Not until I know I'm handling it in the only way that keeps you safe."

Despite the fact he still held her to the ground, she didn't fear he'd hurt her. Griffin would never. She believed that. She trusted it. For the first time, that feeling cemented into her brain. She should've put her faith in him from the beginning.

"The moment you ran my prints, he would've been alerted. He's either already here or on his way. The moment he sees me, he'll kill me."

"Over my dead body."

That was something she didn't want to happen either.

He kissed her again, deeper this time. Telling her with every twist of his lips how much he cared about her.

A throat clearing had Griffin pulling away and looking over his shoulder.

"Can I join the conversation? Maybe we all have a seat at the table?" Juliet chuckled, pointing to said table.

Griffin turned to her again. "You made me a promise. You almost just broke it. Don't do it again."

Then he stood up and held out his hand.

With trembling fingers, she took it.

GRIFFIN WANTED to swing her into his lap but settled for holding hands as they took a seat at the table. He even moved his chair as close to hers as he could get it. Not because he was afraid she'd make another run for it—he'd chase her again. But because he needed to feel her near, to touch her, to make her understand he wasn't going anywhere. No matter what she said, what else he might find out, he would stand proudly by her side.

Was he shocked by the news? Not really. He had an inkling she'd been using a fake name. It was nice to confirm it.

Was he surprised by the missing person's report? Yeah. That one hit him in the gut. He would have to handle that soon. The last thing he wanted was to lose his badge.

"Okay. Let's all take a deep breath. I can get us drinks." Juliet stood up from her chair.

Eve motioned her back down. "I'm not thirsty."

Juliet's butt hit the chair in slow increments as if trying to give Eve as much time as possible before she'd have to tell them her whole story.

They waited. She said nothing.

"Carrington," Juliet started. "The name sounds familiar. A hotel chain or something."

Eve's face flushed red, her eyes darting to the table. Answer enough Juliet was on the right track. He wasn't just sitting next to a woman he'd fallen in love with. He was sitting next to a very rich woman.

"Yes, up and down the Florida coast."

Juliet's fingers fiddled with the end of the folder. "I might've googled a bit. I couldn't help myself. You changed your hair to blonde, but I recognized you in some of the pictures. There were even a few articles about you going missing."

Eve met her gaze. Griffin squeezed her hand to let her know he was there. To take her time. He wasn't going anywhere.

"Your parents died in a plane crash five years ago. I'm sorry."

Griffin was as well, but he wasn't as brave as Juliet to

voice anything yet. Eve was still sitting in the chair and not making a run for it. It seemed like every time he tried to get her to speak, she wanted to run. Better to let his sister take the lead.

"Don't be. I wasn't very close with them." Eve shrugged. "They weren't the most affectionate parents."

At the confession, Griffin moved her hand sitting on the armrests of the chairs connected between them to his lap— the only comfort he could offer at the moment. She didn't pull away, so he took it as a good sign.

"But they were still your parents," Juliet insisted.

"They were two people who provided for me, clothed me, made sure I had a good education. They didn't say they loved me. They didn't say they were proud of me. Was I sad they died? Yes, because I would never wish death on anyone." Eve's voice lowered to a near whisper. "But I was terrified when I found out. Because that's when the nightmare started."

"You have a brother."

Eve nodded.

"Your brother did nothing to stop this man? Who is he?"

Finally, a question Griffin wanted answered. He would've started with that, but he was letting his sister run the show.

Eve trembled, cowering inward. So much so that she tried to pull her hand away. His grip tightened, telling her he wasn't going to budge.

"Juliet," Eve said with a strained breath. "Neither of you completely understand what I'm up against. It's not some man I was in a relationship with. The man always hurting me *is* my brother."

Griffin sucked in a harsh breath. Eve's sorrowful eyes trailed to him.

"You asked if I had any siblings, and I know you think I lied to you saying I was an only child. But in essence, I was. I am. That man is not my brother. He has never shown an ounce of sibling love. Not like you show Juliet. Not like Bryce does either. I'm nothing more than an obstacle in his way."

"To the money your parents left behind?" Juliet asked.

She nodded but didn't leave Griffin's face.

Then she dropped her gaze to the table. "They left us equal shares. I agreed to let him run the hotels because I had no interest in it. I loved working at the bakery in one of the hotels. It was my passion."

"That does not surprise me. No wonder you have magic in your hands." Juliet's tender smile put a short smile on Eve.

They were heading in the right direction. Griffin wanted to see more of her sweet smiles.

"I didn't sign over anything. I wouldn't. He does do some things I don't agree with. He would need my approval with big things he wanted to change. The first time I said no, he hit me so hard I fell, then he kicked me until he cracked a rib. It was the only time I tried to report it. No charges were filed because it was a he said, she said thing. Plus, he had more friends in the police department than I did. Which is zero."

Griffin rubbed his thumb on her hand, trying to soothe her as best as could. He was afraid to move in any other way lest she stop talking.

"His aggression got worse. It got so bad that I stopped working at the bakery. I hid in the house away from the world. I made excuses to my friends why I couldn't go out. I claimed headaches that didn't exist. I told one friend I was hanging with another friend to get out of plans when all I was doing was hiding in my room. I had no one to turn to. No one that would believe me. For the most part, when he did hurt me, it was in places people couldn't see. A few times he'd hit me in the face. I'd use those typical excuses people make to play it off. It got to a point that he wasn't hurting me to get his way, he was doing it because he enjoyed it. It aroused him."

Griffin stiffened. "He didn't..." He couldn't even get the question out.

Eve shook her head, though avoided eye contact. "Not with me, no. He told me all the time how disgusting and poor excuse of a human being I was. But other women, yes. He beat me so badly one night I couldn't move from the floor. One of the maids walked by and didn't see me. But he saw her and..." Eve shivered. "Well, he always takes what he thinks he deserves."

Griffin didn't want to hear any more. It was like opening Pandora's box and regretting the decision the moment the thing popped open.

"The turning point for me," she started in a trance-like voice, "was two days before I fled. I had an actual headache that day. Nothing he did. He brought me a tray of food himself. A simple lunch. Ham sandwich, a bag of chips, and a bottle of water. He was so nice that day. Talking to me like he'd never once laid a hand on me. He said we should start running the company together. No more animosity between us. That I should start coming into the office. I found that very odd. The sudden change in demeanor."

"Well, I'm sure the company has a board of directors. I bet your absence was starting to make waves," Juliet offered.

Eve shrugged. "Maybe. I don't know because I didn't stick around. I didn't touch the food, but one of the maids, Sarah, such a nice woman. I told her to take it away. I wasn't hungry. She looked at it like she wanted it, and I told her to go ahead. She took two bites of the sandwich as she walked out of the room. She didn't make it past the door before she fell, convulsing, and then dying right in front of my eyes."

Griffin couldn't take it. He scooped her out of the chair, placing her on his lap, cocooning her in his arms. Right where she'd always be—if he had his say.

Eve turned her head into his chest, the tears making an appearance. Between the sobs, she said, "Two days later, I ran for my life because I knew if I stayed, my brother would find another way to kill me."

Again, over his dead body, though he didn't repeat it out loud this time.

He'd do anything to protect Eve. When he looked across the table at Juliet, at the hard glint in her eyes, he knew his sister would as well.

The question was, where did they go from here?

9

_____

SHE KNEW her eyes were red-rimmed, but Bryce, who'd arrived a few minutes ago, didn't ask why. He already knew. She felt so exposed, knowing this family knew all her secrets. Her disgusting, disturbing secrets. How pathetic she was. Useless and weak. Letting her brother abuse her for years.

After she'd bawled her eyes out, she left the table and washed her face. When she returned outside, light country music was playing in the background, and Griffin had started the grill. While they'd ambushed her about her secrets, they were now going to turn it into a fun weekend. She didn't think she had it in her to be social. Then Juliet pulled her hand to sit at the table to play cards. Now here they were, thirty minutes later, all sitting around the table acting as if they hadn't imploded her world upside down.

Griffin's chair was still touching hers, his hand on her knee while they waited for Juliet to deal a hand.

"You want me to man the grill?" Bryce asked.

Griffin nodded. "Only because you enjoy doing it."

Meaningless talk. Now they were going to walk on

eggshells with her. She'd confessed every dirty detail, and this was what their relationship had boiled down to.

Juliet's phone rang. She picked it up from the table, groaning. "It's Marcy. I love that woman, but I swear she calls me every weekend with some issue at the cafe that's not an issue."

She stood up from the table, answered the call, and entered the house for privacy.

"It looks like it's ready," Bryce commented, staring at the grill, the charcoal aroma brimming in the air.

"Let me go grab the steaks." Griffin pushed back his chair. "Do you need anything to drink, Eve?"

She shook her head, clasping her hands in her lap. She had no appetite for anything. She was afraid if she ate or drank it would come right back up. Sick to her stomach didn't begin to describe the turmoil going on inside her.

"I can leave if it's weird me being here."

Her eyes popped to Bryce, who wore a tender smile. "I would never ask you to do that."

"Juliet told me what happened and not to say anything to you, but the tension is thick in this yard. It's worse than the humidity. I don't want to make you feel uncomfortable."

Oh, this family. This wonderful, kind family. How had she gotten so lucky to move to a small town right next to the perfect man whose whole family welcomed her with open arms?

"I want you to stay. It wouldn't be the same without you."

Bryce's smile widened. "The same could be said about you. You're a wonderful addition to the family."

"Well, I—"

Bryce shook his head. "Nope, I have to stop whatever protest is about to come out. You are a part of this family. No negotiations."

But was she? What happened if things between her and Griffin didn't work out?

"Things between Griffin and I aren't..." Serious? Were they? She didn't know how to describe what was between them. They hadn't even slept together yet. Just kisses here and there. "We're only....it's not..." She frowned, hating how she couldn't find the right words.

Bryce chuckled. "No matter what might or might not develop between you two, you're stuck with us. That's final." Bryce leaned forward. "But between me and you, Grif is a goner. He's not a PDA kind of guy, and there's not a moment I haven't seen him keep his hands off you."

She couldn't hide her smile. To think she brought that out of him.

"I don't know the full story. You don't need to tell me. Neither does Jules or Grif," Bryce said, shaking his head. "But you're not alone anymore. I'm not just talking about us Stuarts. I mean the whole town. One phone call from me to Judge Riner and your brother won't be allowed to step foot in this town."

"But...how?"

A plate of juicy steaks landed on the table with a soft thud. Griffin sat back down, grabbing her hands into his lap.

"An order of protection, for starters. He hurt you, and in this town, that doesn't fly." Griffin's hold on her increased. "Every officer will have a picture of him so the first sign of him, he'll be pulled over and asked to leave."

Her stomach twisted with unease. "I don't want the whole town to know about this."

"It's time to stop hiding," Griffin said with a tight jaw. As if he were mad at her? He had said he wasn't.

"I've been hiding my whole life. From reporters. From people wanting something from me. Money. Status. A nice room for free. I don't have friends. I have people in my life who use me and pretend to be my friend for what I can offer them. I can't just stop doing something I've been doing my entire life because you say so, Griffin."

His expression softened, as did the grip on her hands. "This town might be in everyone's business, but they also ban together when necessary. No one is going to treat you any differently."

Eve pulled at her hands so hard her chair wobbled backward, forcing Griffin to let go and grab ahold of it. It was enough to get her freedom. She stood up and backed away.

"You're already treating me differently. I cry and then it's like nothing happened. It's like I didn't pour my heart out. Bryce comes and we're playing cards and going to grill."

Griffin stood up, though didn't approach her. "How is that treating you differently? We did the same thing last week."

Well, that was true. But it felt different. Like Bryce had said, the tension in the air was palpable.

"It just feels different to me."

"Because there's no secrets between us anymore. That's a good thing, Eve."

"There's still a few."

Griffin's eyes narrowed. "Then let's get them out in the open. We're done with secrets. We have to be."

"Or what?"

What was she doing? Why couldn't she sit down and enjoy a nice steak with potato salad and whatever else was on the menu?

A muscle in his cheek bunched as he clenched his teeth. Yeah, she was purposely trying to upset him and she had no idea why. Maybe because it would be easier to flee if he hated her. Didn't he understand that a little piece of paper wasn't going to keep her brother away from her? Too much money was at stake. Too much power he wanted, and she stood in the way.

"Or I'll take you over my knee and spank you. That's what."

Bryce chuckled, then coughed, turning it into a weird snort as if he hadn't meant to react at all.

She didn't know what to say to that either. Her body, on the other hand, sizzled with desire at the thought of his hands anywhere on her.

Griffin shook his head, groaning. "No, I won't. I don't know why I said that. I would never hurt you. Not even like that."

Well, the way he had said it didn't sound painful. More erotic than anything else.

"I don't know how to alleviate your fear. I imagine it will take a while, and I understand that. Don't push me away, Eve. Whatever you're doing right now, don't do that to me. We're in this together. We'll figure this out together. Starting with an order of protection—"

"He's not going to listen to a dumb piece of paper!"

"But at least there's a paper trail. You're going to have to do something about him. You can't look over your shoulder your entire life."

"I planned to."

Griffin grimaced. "Not anymore. Not with me."

"Stop telling me what to do."

Eve caught Bryce bobbing his head back and forth between them, relaxed in his chair as if the conversation wasn't an intense one. It almost made her laugh. If it wasn't Griffin putting her at ease at times, it was another one of the Stuart siblings doing it.

"What's your plan then, Eve? To run? To run forever?" He exhaled as if admitting defeat. "To run from me?"

The thought of running from him gutted her. Yet, her feet ached to move toward the exit. It's what she knew. It's all she ever did. Run from problems instead of facing them head-on.

"I don't know how not to run."

"Then I'll help teach you." He held out his hand. "Trust me that I won't let you fall in the process."

He had yet to do so. Always catching her in her moment of need.

She took two steps and placed her hand inside his. He pulled her closer until she was wrapped in his warm embrace.

His lips hit her neck and his warm breath teased her ear. "Later, you can tell me these other secrets. When we're alone. Because when it comes to me and you, I want nothing hidden."

Well, the last secret she had was a doozy. She didn't know how she'd confess it.

"So...should I start grilling the steaks or wait?"

She peeked at Bryce, her lips turning up at his silly grin.

It wouldn't be easy, but this family would teach her how not to run for once.

JULIET HAD LEFT SHORTLY after the phone call. A true emergency from Marcy for once. A pipe burst in the kitchen. Bryce grilled and enjoyed a few card games with them and then left. Eve helped Griffin clean up, even loading the dishwasher. As he came in from outside watching her at his counter putting a plate in the device, he wondered how he'd get her to stay—forever.

He knew deep in his gut she was *the one*. He suspected that feeling had been there from the first moment he met her. She'd not only smacked into his chest but shoved in the idea that was now lingering in his mind every moment of each day.

But now that the truth of her identity was out, he had to tread even more carefully. He was up against a lot. Not just a psychotic brother who wanted to kill her.

She was rich.

She was more than a small-town girl.

She was one of those women who would always be unattainable.

Yet, she was his Eve. Sweet, shy smiles. Glowering when the next Christmas tune always came on in the cafe. He figured she didn't know she reacted that way. He'd have to ask her why she didn't like Christmas. And hating Christmas, why she moved to a town that threw it in your face every day of the year?

She was close to breaking. The one he feared the most. One wrong move and he'd lose her. Forever. The wrong kind of forever he was looking for.

He moved closer, and when she turned around from the dishwasher, she jumped as he knew she would, startled by his presence. It gave him the opportunity to wrap his arm around her waist and catch her.

He would always catch her.

"Do you know how much I love seeing you put things away or grab something that requires you to bend?"

She grinned, her eyes brimming with laughter. "No, how much?"

"Way too much." Then he dipped his head and kissed her.

His lips melded with hers as if they were one. Her low moan filled the air and made the ache in his chest disappear. Most times, he worried he'd do the wrong thing. Little evidence like that told him he'd done the right thing.

Her hands that were stuck between them slithered up his chest, eliciting a delightful shiver from him. Damn, he needed her in every way.

"Stay with me."

"Sure, you want to watch a movie or something?"

His lips found her chin this time, pressing light kisses until he hit her neck. He ran his tongue to her ear, taking a nibble.

"No, I mean stay with me. Tonight. All night long."

Instead of her hands running another path down his chest, they pushed on him. He let go of her, never wanting her to feel like he was trapping her.

"I don't think that's a good idea."

"I have two reasons why I think it's a good idea."

She crossed her arms, nodding. "Okay, let's hear them."

He held up a finger. "I don't care where we stay, your house or mine, but I don't want to leave you alone. Not if you think he could be in town or on his way."

A shiver rippled across her body, her eyes widening with the fear he hated witnessing.

"While I will sleep on the couch, I'd much prefer it in a bed. Next to you. Reason number one. To make sure you're safe and comfortable. And fear nothing."

Her arms dropped to her sides. "And reason number two?"

He was now doubting he should've voiced there were two reasons. He should've kept the second one to himself.

But he had said no more secrets between them, and that included him.

"Because I want to show you how much you mean to me. I want to kiss every spot on your body and remove the memories that have no place there. I want to pleasure you until you're so sated with bliss that you never want to walk away from me."

Her eyes widened at his candid words. But he figured they were better than the other three little words. I love you. That he sensed would've had her running for the door.

Of course, by the fright in her eyes, these words might be having the same reaction.

"Griffin..." The rest of whatever she wanted to say stalled on her lips. Then her eyes cast downward as Walter rubbed against her leg.

Saved by a cat.

The moment had nearly turned disastrous because he couldn't hold back his emotions.

"Or we can watch a movie or something."

He'd said too much. Gone too far too soon.

She bit her bottom lip as her eyes lifted to his once again. Walter still circled her feet as if sensing she needed comfort.

"I guess this is a good time to confess my last secret."

Whatever it was he could handle it. Hell, he thought he'd handled everything else pretty damn well thus far. She'd been lying to him since the moment he met her. Other people would've taken offense to that. Would've shoved her out of their life. He only wanted to pull her deeper into his.

"I've never..." Her eyes glided back to Walter, her cheeks blooming a deep red. "I've never been with a man before. I'm twenty-seven years old and I'm a virgin."

He exhaled a slow breath, after holding it waiting for a blow that would crush him. Everything she'd said earlier would've brought him to his knees if he hadn't been sitting down. But this confession? This was nothing compared to anything else she had said. If anything, he relished the idea he'd be the first man to love her thoroughly. The only man —if he had his way.

"I'm thirty-three years old and have only been with two women in my life. I guess you can call me a novice as much as you."

She flinched at his admission. "You're just saying that."

"Why would I lie about something like that?"

She drew a hand up and down, pointing at him, shaking her head. "Because you're you. You're the sexiest man in this town. The purest gentleman I've ever met. Kind to everyone you meet. A smile to die for. The softest touch imaginable. You're a prime catch, and I find it hard to believe you've only been with two women."

His heart swelled with pride at her comments. At the way she thought of him. That had to be an excellent sign that he'd be able to keep her forever in his life.

"Well, it's true. I thought I'd marry my high school sweetheart, Holly. She was my first. Me, hers. We talked about our future and how many kids we'd have. I had always planned to become a cop. She wanted to eventually become the principal of our school. We went to the same college. We were inseparable until I moved back to town and she decided living here was not in her plans anymore. That *I* wasn't in her plans anymore. That broke me. It shook my entire core belief in relationships. I threw myself into work and made the chief of police at age twenty-eight. It's a small town. It wasn't that hard as it could've been in a larger one. I settled into my position and felt more confident about myself for the first time in a long time. I started dating a woman a town over. When I thought things were getting serious, I invited her to move in. Take things to another level. She opened my eyes that she could never live here, surrounded by Christmas twenty-four-seven. Same as Holly. I guess, after that, I got gun-shy about women and my ability to keep them by my side."

Her gaze filtered back to the floor as if telling him she fell into that same category. That, no matter what he did, he wouldn't be able to keep her by his side either.

Well, he was willing to take the risk. To put his heart on the line again, even if the odds were stacked astronomically against him.

"I don't want to screw this up."

She read his mind. He didn't want to screw anything up either.

Her eyes lifted back to his.

"I screw up everything I touch. I can't do anything rig—"

"Stop it!" he hollered. "Don't you dare speak about yourself like that. Don't you dare take his words as gospel."

Damn it. He frightened her by raising his voice. He hated the way she took a step back and cowered her shoulders.

His tone softened to a near whisper. "You're perfect. In every possible way. If you think for one minute I believe anything like that about you, then you haven't been paying attention to me."

Her body relaxed, the tension draining from her features. Then she walked closer and placed a hand over his heart. It beat erratically and he needed her to feel that. To know he was terrified as much as her.

"I'm scared, Griffin."

He didn't move, even though he wanted to wrap his arms

around her. He knew she was still on the verge of turning away from him.

"Doesn't the beat of my heart tell you how scared I am as well?"

"I'm scared I'm not as strong as you think I am. I want you. I want to...stay the night." She sighed. "But I don't want to hurt you in the end, because I'm a coward. You want me to do things I might not ever be able to do. I don't think I can confront him."

This was progress. He'd take baby steps over no steps at all.

Would he be picking up the pieces of his heart down the road? High possibility. But he'd take the risk. He'd take any part of her he could get. When he could get it.

"I'm going to prove you wrong. I'm going to show you how strong you truly are. In the meantime, I'm going to love you like you deserve to be loved. So..." He put his hands on her waist, jutting her closer so her body grazed his. "Your house or mine?"

10

Was she doing the right thing?

As Griffin's lips devoured hers, she knew in her heart she was. This man was the kindest, tenderest man she'd ever met. Deep down she knew he'd never hurt her. Putting her trust in him was one of the hardest things she'd ever done. But she did. She was.

She broke the kiss, breathing heavily. When she hadn't answered his question, he kissed her as if that would pull the answer out of her. It worked.

"Yours." Her eyes grazed to his lips. "Now."

The devilish grin on his lips said she was in for a magical night. He swung her into his arms, eliciting a delighted giggle from her.

Then he was depositing her on his bed after walking faster than she'd ever seen him do before.

"Don't move." His grin inched up even higher. "Well, you can get naked, but don't get out of that bed. I'll be right back."

He left the room.

She wondered where he was going when she heard little

beeps echo her way. Setting the alarm. Okay. She under-stood now. They were retiring for the evening, and he wanted to make sure everything was secure.

She shimmied out of her pants and tossed her shirt off, throwing both articles to the floor. Cool air rushed across her skin, making her shiver. Her hands wove around to her back, her fingers grazing the clasp to her bra. She shivered again. This time from nerves.

She wasn't clueless when it came to what happened between a man and a woman. Just because she'd never done this before didn't mean she didn't know what to expect. Of course, it also didn't mean it made her comfortable to think of getting completely naked. She'd never been naked in front of anyone before.

Now that she was alone, her thoughts to run amuck, she wasn't sure this was the brightest idea. Sure, he confessed to being with only two women, but that was two more people than she'd ever been with.

Growing up, life hadn't been easy. Trusting anyone. The few she did trust, she never had any passing attraction to them.

Startled at the noise, she dropped her hands, her eyes darting to the door. Griffin stood in the doorway, a sweet smile on his face. He held something in his hands that when he moved in the slightest, it crinkled.

Condoms.

Oh boy, this was happening.

Maybe the panic lit up her face because he dashed to the bed, tossing the packages to the nightstand, and cradled her cheek.

"We can wait. Nothing needs to happen. I can even sleep in the living room. But what I don't want is you frightened. Not of me."

His warm hand heated the parts of her body that had frozen from her worry. All the doubts that had attacked her in his absence slipped away. Well, most of them. A few lingering doubts held her captive.

"I want this. I'm..." She leaned into his hand pressing against her cheek, closing her eyes. "I don't want to mess this up. I already am."

A soft kiss hit her forehead. "We need to work on your confidence. You're not messing anything up."

Her eyes gradually opened. The first thing she saw was the patience in his gaze. His hand still touched her cheek, stroking, calming the last remaining nerves.

That's right.

She was safe with Griffin. If she asked him to stop at any time, he would. She had nothing to fear from him.

This she knew without a doubt.

The fear didn't stem from him hurting her. Even from the beginning when she first met him, her instincts had screamed that he wouldn't harm her.

No, this fear frightened her even more than physical pain.

The moment she took this leap, connected as one with him, she feared she'd never want to leave. That the feeling she'd developed for him would run even deeper. And in the end, she knew it would never work out between them. Not when he expected her to confront her brother.

She'd never be brave enough for that.

But she couldn't resist the temptation in front of her. One touch. That's all it took from him to have her walls come crumbling down. Her worries to dissipate. She was doing this, and she'd protect the memories at all costs. Because sooner or later that's all she'd have.

"Why are you still dressed?" she whispered.

"I have no idea." His grin made her heart skip a beat.

Then he stood, undressing so fast she whined inside that she couldn't enjoy the show a little longer. His body was lean and toned from head to toe. She couldn't wait to touch him, roam her hands around his chest. Feel the ridges and planes.

His cock stood at attention, pulsating with need. Her eyes rounded when she caught sight of it. There was no way he'd fit inside her.

"Are you done ogling me? Because I like the way you look at me, but now you have me nervous with the way your eyes bulged out."

She giggled, turning away, embarrassed and afraid to voice anything. When he joined her on the bed and touched her shoulders, she met his gaze.

"You're...ummm..."

His hand ran down her arm. "Yes? I'm what?"

She bit her lip, unable to hold back the smile trying to break free. "You're quite..." She closed her eyes, cringing at her embarrassment. "Griffin, you're never going to fit in me."

Her eyes remained closed, but his laughter was loud and clear. Another sweet kiss hit her forehead. Then he was lowering her to the bed.

"I have no doubts we're going to fit perfectly together."

Before she could open her eyes at his bold words, hot breath hit below, above her panties. Now she was afraid to open them. His hands glided her panties off, then she braced for it. His cock to touch her, shove inside her.

Instead, a soft kiss hit her where her panties had been. She arched off the bed at the erotic touch.

"Griffin..."

He didn't stop to respond, his mouth and tongue doing the most amazing things she never knew were possible.

Just as he was in everything else he did in life, he bestowed upon her body as well. Gentle. Soft. Thorough. He licked, sucked, and stroked her until she felt herself meeting his movement with her own. Up and down her hips went as he pulled emotions out of her she'd never felt before.

Tingles radiated around her body, telling her she knew what was coming. She may have never been with a man before, but it didn't mean she'd never given herself an orgasm. The one making its way to the surface would be the strongest she'd ever felt.

"Oh, Griffin..." she whispered, her hands finding the top of his head as she still hadn't managed to open her eyes.

She stroked his hair as he did the same to her until finally it peaked. Moaning his name, digging her nails in his head so he wouldn't move, she came.

His body smoothed a path up hers until wet lips hit her neck.

"I want to hear you say my name over and over like that. So damn beautiful."

She finally opened her eyes, the passion blaring in his. "Love me. Give me more of that."

"Your wish is my command."

Then he grabbed one of the packages from the night-stand, ripping it open. It didn't take long for him to roll it on. Then he positioned himself, holding still.

"I don't want to hurt you, but it might at first. I will go slow."

Her hands wrapped around his neck, pulling him closer until their lips touched. "I trust you with all my heart."

He nodded, pushing against her entrance. Their lips met once again as he slowly worked his way inside. She'd never felt such pain and pleasure mixed together. Parts hurt, he stretched her so much. In the same breath, it felt divine the farther he went.

When he was seated fully inside, he stopped, pulling away his lips and bending his head to the pillow. His heavy breaths mingled with hers filled the room.

Her hand slid down his back, eliciting a tremble from him. "Are you okay?"

His lips pressed against her neck. "Yes. I need a moment. You feel so damn good, I'm afraid I'm going to explode before I can even move."

The thought she had him at her mercy had her mouth twisting up into a wicked smile. She'd get him to the edge of madness as he had done for her. She pumped her hips up, relishing in the harsh intake of breath he let loose.

"Eve..." he warned, lifting his head. "Give me one more moment."

She wrapped her legs around his waist, pushing him even farther inside as a groan slipped from his lips. "It feels so wonderful. Let go. It's okay." Her eyes glided to the nightstand then back to him in a flash. "You obviously planned for more than one round. This is only the beginning."

"You're not getting any sleep tonight."

Then he crushed his lips to hers as he ground into her, pumping in and out as if someone had slapped his ass to get him moving. In between the bliss spreading around her body once again, she realized it was she who had done so. Her legs were wrapped tightly around him, her hands digging into his ass, urging him on. He honestly didn't need any encouragement as he pounded in and out of her. Each thrust sent a bolt of lust through her, making her ache for more.

She knew the moment was coming to an end when he broke the kiss, his face twisting in ecstasy, his body tensing.

She relaxed her body, her hands traveling slowly up his back as he rested his head next to her, his heavy body still on top of her. She had no desire for him to move.

A feather-light kiss hit her neck.

No words hit his lips though. She didn't need any. His touch, his movements, the way he made love to her told her everything.

She was safe in his arms.

She'd be filled with love.

As long as she stuck around.

HE INHALED the wonderful aroma of vanilla, a scent that always lingered on her. Then he wrapped his arms around her, his hands splayed around her stomach in a deadlock. Then his lips caressed her neck. God, what he wouldn't give to haul her back to his bedroom and not leave for a week. Unfortunately, the real world had intruded, and they couldn't continue to live in the bubble they'd erected this past weekend.

Saturday had been filled with so many harrowing emotions. Sadness, pain, rage.

Pleasure, desire, love.

Sunday had been even better than the day before. Nothing terrible entered their space. Only the touch of his hands covering every inch of her, branding her, marking her with his love. She should have no doubt how much he cared about her. How much he never wanted her to leave. Though that sentiment never left his mouth. He'd have to tread carefully.

Like right now.

She was due at the cafe in thirty minutes, and he had to

start his own shift. But before all of that, they had to take care of something important. Something he knew she wouldn't want to do.

"Don't start that now," she said breathlessly as he placed a few more kisses on her neck until he trailed to her ear where he nibbled.

"Start what? I'm not doing anything."

She giggled, opening her neck some more to give him better access. Oh, yes. She wanted him as much as he craved her.

He pressed more light kisses to her neck before he forced himself to stop. If he kept going in this direction, they'd both be calling out sick to work.

She must've felt the change in him when he lifted his head, but he didn't let go of her.

"I think—"

She twisted in his arms, cutting off his sentence. Her hands pressed against his chest, and he froze, waiting for her to push him away. Instead, she slid them down a fraction, then paused.

"Don't say anything. Please."

"Eve, we can't ignore it. We did all day yesterday, but today we can't."

She tensed as if he were going to hit her or something. God, he hated that reaction but understood it. She'd been bullied and pushed around her entire life. First by her parents and then by her brother. She'd never had a say in anything, and now he was about to do the same thing. He hated to do that to her, but it was important they took action before her brother did.

"There's a missing person's report on you. I have to take care of that."

A tremble touched her body. His hands were settled on

her waist, and as much as he wanted to move them, pull her closer, they remained where they were. He needed her to know she was in control. That he wouldn't overpower her or give the appearance he wanted to overpower her at all.

"After we fix that, we'll file an order of protection."

She shook her head frantically, her lips pressing together as if forcing a scream to stay hidden.

"I will not let him hurt you. I will not let him get near you. Let me help you. Let me show you how strong I know you are." His grip strengthened but not enough to hurt. "A woman who runs and hides as well as she did is strong. Make no mistake about that."

Her eyes lifted to his, parts of her relaxing.

That's right.

He needed to remind her of all the things she had already done on her own. Of all the ways she had displayed her courage.

"You got away. You outsmarted that asshole."

A short smile peeked through.

"You moved to a town that celebrates a holiday you don't care for."

She gasped, her hands gripping his shirt. "What are you talking about?"

He grinned. "Sweetheart, I notice everything about you because I can never take my eyes off you. I see when a new Christmas song comes on and you can barely control not rolling your eyes. And when you see some of the decorations displayed around town, the disgust on your lips is faint but it's there. You hate Christmas. Yet you endure it because you're strong."

"I thought I hid that well."

"You did, just not with me." He wanted to ask why she

hated Christmas, but he didn't want to get sidetracked from a more important issue.

"It's not just Christmas. I don't care for any holiday."

"Not even Halloween? Valentine's? Easter? Everyone loves the Easter Bunny."

A sweet but short chuckle left her lips. "Not this girl. Holidays were faked in my family. For the press, it looked like my parents adored us and adored celebrating whatever rolled around. Behind closed doors, nothing was celebrated. Nothing was special. I came to learn those days meant nothing but how good it made us look if we outdid everyone else in presentation and style."

"I'm sorry for everything you ever endured. It is now my life mission for you to fall in love with the Easter Bunny."

He didn't know if it was the way he said it, so seriously, or the determined twist of his lips, but she burst out laughing.

"Why the Easter Bunny?"

"Because that's my favorite holiday. I love that furry rabbit."

She dropped her head to his chest, giggling. The sound filled up his soul. That's all he wanted to hear. Her happiness. For her to feel safe.

Her fingers tightened on his shirt, her nails digging into his skin. The lighthearted moment was over.

"I don't want to go to jail, Griffin. I can't bear to see you put handcuffs on me."

He flinched, pulling her head up to look at him. "What the hell are you talking about?"

"My fake ID."

He let out a huge breath, smiling. "I'm not going to arrest you. I'm sure once we explain to Judge Riner the circumstances, it won't matter what you did."

She stiffened. "And if he doesn't understand?"

"Do you trust me?"

There was a long moment of silence and then she nodded.

"Then take my word for it that it's all going to be okay. No one is going to arrest you. No one, especially your brother, is going to touch you ever again."

She nodded again, then slipped out of his embrace. He couldn't force her to remain where she was. He needed her to know that he'd never force anything on her. That she was in control.

"I'm going to freshen up."

He let her walk out of the kitchen and finished making the sandwiches she had been working on before he ruined the mood. They left ten minutes later. He'd called Juliet for Eve, letting her know she'd be a little late to work. Juliet had assumed so already.

The first thing he did was contact the issuing agency who put out the missing person's report. After assuring the detective Evelyn Carrington was alive and well—with her voicing the same—he said he'd take care of everything on his end.

Though the order of protection hadn't been issued yet, he told the detective to let her brother know he wasn't welcome in her life anymore. Griffin had no doubt the man would contact her brother right away. That had thrown the detective for a second, but he understood.

Griffin doubted that. If what Eve said was true, then that man was probably paid by her brother to look the other way on way too many things. Not just things that involved her.

Their next stop was to see Judge Riner. Griffin started the conversation, explaining everything. Judge Riner sat stoically in his chair, his hands on top of each other on his round belly as he spoke. No emotion. No expression. No idea what he was thinking. But Griffin wasn't worried because he knew Judge Riner was a fair and honest man.

"Have you asked for a police report on the maid's death, Griffin?"

"Not yet, your honor. I have a feeling I won't get very far with the police there."

"I'm not lying. I swear," Eve pleaded, though her eyes were cast downward.

Griffin held eye contact with the judge so he could see the compassionate smile he wore, unlike Eve.

"Ms. Carrington, look at me."

Eve slowly raised her head to face the judge.

"I didn't ask Griffin that because I don't believe you. But if that poor woman was murdered, your brother should pay the crime for it. Don't you agree?"

She gave him a tight nod.

"Not that Griffin has jurisdiction there. Call anyway. See what they say. I'll have an order of protection issued and served to him immediately. No contact in any form with you. Must remain a thousand feet away and hand in any firearms he possesses."

"You'd do all that for me?"

Judge Riner's smile softened at Eve's trembling question. "I don't take kindly to abusive men. Ask Griffin about his sister's ex-husband. No one should live in fear, Ms. Carrington. I can see how afraid you are. You're safe in our town. We protect our residents. You are a part of this community, right?"

"Yes. I love it here."

"Then you have nothing to fear."

Eve stood and held out her hand. "Thank you, your honor. Truly, thank you."

Judge Riner stood as well, clasping her hand in both of his. "There's no thanks when I'm doing my job."

She bit her lip when he let go of her hand. "I'm sorry for the fake ID. For lying."

"Again, you have nothing to fear. Griffin will make sure of that." Judge Riner sat down. "I wouldn't mind if you held a few extra goodies that you bake today for me. I do love your sweets."

"Of course, your honor."

The smile she displayed lasted all the way out of the building and to the front of the cafe. She threw her arms around him.

"Thank you, Grif. I wouldn't have been able to do any of this without you."

"Yes, you could've. But thankfully, you'll never have to find out because I'm always going to be here."

Then he placed a kiss on her neck, before finding her lips and telling her with one passionate kiss how true his words were.

She was not alone. Not anymore.

11

As the day drew on, the nerves and fear that had coiled tight like a snake around her spine slowly ebbed away. It wasn't hard when everyone made her feel protected. Though having everyone know her business wasn't something she liked.

Small towns. Now she knew.

Since the moment Griffin dropped her off at work, she'd gotten words of encouragement from everyone who came in. Unfortunately, Chip had called out with a stomach bug and Tabitha had as well. They had attended the same party yesterday, something Eve was grateful Griffin declined for them. Juliet hadn't attended either, luckily. She manned the kitchen while Eve handled the front counter. They were doing their best to stay sane around the chaos. Eve feared *she* was the reason they were so packed.

There was finally a moment of peace for her to catch her breath. Her mind wandered to all the comforting words from the townsfolk.

"Now that I know you're not actually blonde, I see you.

You're definitely Evelyn Carrington. Always thought you were so pretty. Still are as a blonde," Mrs. Donavan had said.

Mr. Pitts' determined grin had matched every word. "That asshole steps foot in town he'll be stepping right back out. You got my word if I see him."

"I always thought he looked like a douche. Real douche smile he has," Tonya from the salon had punctuated with a severe frown.

"I thought you had looked familiar. I just knew it." Bob had snapped his fingers, still disgustingly dirty as usual when he came in, making her flinch. "Of course, if I see that jerk, I'll stand up for you. You're safe here."

"I own a gun if you need it. Won't say a word to anyone. Not even the chief," Gary from the hardware store had said, leaning in close as he whispered. "Or better yet, I'll use it for you."

"We got your back. The whole football team. We'll crush him for you," Teddy, the star quarterback had even said.

His comment most of all had warmed her heart. Even the teenagers in town wanted to protect her. She thought she'd picked the perfect town because he'd never find her here. Instead, she found the perfect town that accepted her for her. Not what she represented. Not one person had commented on her money or status. If she could get them a free room in one of her hotels. How she could make them look good in the press. It had all been about how they'd protect her from the evilness that had ruled her life for so long.

"Eve!"

She jumped, putting a hand to heart when she turned to Juliet, who wore a silly grin.

"You didn't answer me. Sorry," Juliet said, "I had to scream your name."

A trembling giggle fell out. "I was lost in thought."

Juliet's expression softened. "Everyone been okay? Not too in your face, I hope."

Oh, they'd been in her face. Chatting and commenting, even if she would've protested. While Juliet had looked chagrined for making her work the counter, Eve figured this was Juliet's way to show her that not only did she, Bryce, and Griffin have her back, but so did everyone else. And she wouldn't believe it unless she saw it with her own eyes. Well, they were wide open.

"A little bit, but it's been a good day. I didn't expect so many people to..." She shrugged. "To care."

Juliet wrapped an arm around her, pulling her into her side. "Once you're a part of this community, we stick together."

"Thanks for letting me see that for my own eyes."

"I'm glad you're not mad at me. I wasn't trying to make you feel bad or out of place."

They pulled away from each other.

"You don't have to stick around until closing. I can handle it."

Eve shook her head. "I got here late. I will close with you. That's final. How are Chip and Tabitha feeling?"

A sigh of relief hit Juliet's features. "Much better. They both said they'll be back tomorrow."

"Good." Eve looked around, anywhere but at Juliet. "I'd like to go back to normal. Not pretend like everything is the same, but I don't want to be treated differently. With kids gloves or anything."

"Won't happen."

She looked at Juliet. The sharp gleam in her eye said she was telling the truth.

"Everyone said what they wanted to say today, and tomorrow will be like it never happened. Trust me. I lived through it myself."

Eve was coming to learn to trust her. To trust everyone in town. How could she not? They made it difficult to ignore them. To see the faith in their eyes they'd be by her side every step of the way.

Night came quickly, just as busy near closing. When Griffin came to pick her up, since they drove to town together, he even helped close the cafe. He pulled into his driveway, glancing at her house before settling on her.

"My house or yours?"

"Yours."

She wasn't ready to be alone. Though she knew he wouldn't leave her alone. But despite that, she felt safer in his house. The reminder of those odd incidents still echoed in her mind. He hadn't forgotten either.

"I'm going to dust for prints around the windowsill in your room. Is that okay?"

"If you think it's necessary."

"Just to be safe."

They headed for the kitchen where Griffin grabbed two plates from the cupboard and set them on the table. She unloaded the food from the bag she'd taken home from the cafe. They divided out the food, yet neither made a move to eat.

"Have you heard from him? I know he was served the protection order."

She shivered. So Darrian officially knew where she was and that he wasn't welcome near her. His wrath would be insane.

"Eve?" Griffin reached out his hand.

She grasped it, unable to meet his eyes. He'd see the fear embedded in them. "No, I haven't. You know I don't have a cell phone yet, and I haven't been home to check the messages on the house phone."

She'd told herself to get a cell phone. Griffin had even suggested it before he knew the truth, always chuckling at her that she didn't like technology. It hadn't been that. She didn't want to lie everywhere she went. Use her fake identity when she didn't have to. She'd survived the last two months without a cell phone. It hadn't been that hard. Even in her old life, she had never been big on social media. She already had the media following her around without her consent. So why put herself out there even more when the world didn't need to know every aspect of her life?

"We should fix that. You should have a phone on you at all times. In case of an emergency."

She hated the thought of needing to call him in a panic. Her body betrayed her, making her tremble. His grip tightened.

"I'll look into it."

"We can go together tomorrow."

She smiled at the way he said it so innocently as if he wasn't doing it to keep her safe, but because he wanted to spend as much time with her as he could. She knew better. Though she'd take his protectiveness because it was new and refreshing.

"Can we go to my house when we're done eating? I need some clothes."

"I'll do the window while you pack."

This time his hand trembled and she tightened her grip in comfort. He made it sound like she was moving in when that wasn't a subject they had touched. She could tell he regretted saying it.

"I'll check my messages as well."

She decided to ignore it. They weren't ready for that level of talk. She had no idea if she'd even stay in town. Darrian might not have reached out yet, but he would. He'd make her life a living hell until she had no choice but to run again.

Griffin must've sensed where her thoughts had taken her because he leaned closer, pressing his lips to hers.

"We're in this together. Everything. Remember that." The kiss deepened. "Remember the promise you made as well."

She would never forget. Because leaving was always in the recesses of her mind. Problem was he knew that as well.

GRIFFIN CALLED Duke to come get the few prints he pulled from Eve's windowsill in her bedroom. After packing up his equipment, he joined her in the living room.

"So? Any messages on the machine?"

She shook her head, her forehead creased.

"Well, I'd say that's a good thing. He knows to follow the order."

She pierced him with a severe look. "He's not an idiot. Leaving a message would prove he'd violated it. And my brother is no idiot."

The asshole was in Griffin's eyes, but he didn't think starting an argument about that would be wise.

"Duke should be here soon to take the prints I found."

"You won't find his." She turned away, walking toward the kitchen.

"Maybe not, but if you think someone was in here, then I'm going to investigate it. It's my job." *And I care about you too much not to do anything.* Though he kept that to himself.

He was treading in deep waters with her. The slightest wrong move and he'd drown. He knew it without even thinking about it. Every moment that went by, he knew she teetered on the edge of running, even with him trying to reassure her he'd keep her safe.

A whisper of a smile appeared before flickering away as she grabbed a glass from the cupboard. "I know. If it makes you feel better to do it, then I want you to."

Why the hell didn't it make her feel better as well? What was she afraid he'd find?

She poured herself a glass of water, sipping it.

The tension in the house grew as they stared at each other. He had no idea how it'd gotten as thick as it had when they'd been fine before coming over here.

"Tomorrow, besides the phone, we'll call an alarm company to come out and install it in here."

"I'd have to call Mindy first."

He grinned. "It'll be fine. I promise."

The glass made a sharp sound as it hit the counter. "Maybe so, but I'd feel better calling Mindy before installing something. The owner might not appreciate me doing something without permission."

"He won't have an issue with it. It's something that should've been done a long time ago."

She frowned. "Who owns this house?"

The sheepish grin he delivered told her without voicing anything.

She shook her head, laughing. "Why didn't you tell me you owned this place? All that stuff in the shed is yours. You never had the intention of bringing any of it to the donation center."

Well, eventually, he would've. It hadn't been a pressing matter.

"I didn't think it was a big deal that I rented this place out. And why should any of this"—he asked waving his hand at the furniture she had taken from the shed— "sit and collect dust when it's now getting used?"

"I'm not a charity case. I don't want to be treated like one."

He inhaled, then exhaled, trying to find the right words. "Why are we fighting?"

She blinked as if surprised by the question.

"Because I feel like we're fighting about silly things." He took a few steps toward her but stopped before getting into her space. He didn't want to make her feel trapped. "I'm scared too, you know. I'm scared you'll eventually leave and not at the hands of your brother. Of your own accord."

Her eyes darted to the counter, confirming the thought had crossed her mind.

"But it doesn't mean we need to argue about these kind of things because we're scared. We'll muddle through this together. Like we agreed earlier."

He wanted to rush to her side and force her to look at him, yet he stood frozen in his spot, waiting with bated breath. She finally granted his wish, meeting his gaze. A tentative smile emerged. Before she could respond, a knock sounded on the door.

"That's probably Duke. Why don't you pack a bag, and we'll go back to my house."

He turned without waiting for a response. Duke retrieved the prints he'd pulled from the windowsill and left as quickly as he arrived. Eve packed a small duffle bag, showing Griffin she had no intention of spending every night at his house. That was fine. He didn't mind sleeping at her house some nights.

The rest of the evening was pleasant, as if they hadn't spoken one harsh word to each other. They woke up with laughter and sunshine. When he told her he'd call the alarm company, she didn't protest. Perhaps the conversation had helped last night.

A whole week passed with nothing happening besides Eve getting a cell phone, an alarm on the house, and them taking turns where they slept. Darrian didn't reach out, not even via a lawyer to protest the order. Griffin wasn't sure what to make of that, but he knew it put Eve on edge. As long as she didn't leave town, she'd be safe. While he couldn't be around her twenty-four-seven, everyone else in town had her back.

The prints he'd pulled from her windowsill had proven to be useless. Only Eve's prints came back. Which meant nobody had broken in and touched it, or they had used gloves. Griffin wasn't sure which one he believed more, but since Eve didn't appear too concerned about it any longer, he chose to put it on the back burner. For now.

"Hey, Chief, Darlene's having problems again."

Griffin looked up from his desk to see Sherry standing in the doorway to his office. "How bad?"

"Well, she says Dicky is drunk again and making a scene in the yard since she won't let him in the house."

Griffin stood up, shoving the papers he'd been working on in a folder and to the side. "I'll take a ride over there."

They had two officers on duty every shift, but he had to assume they were busy with other things if Sherry wanted him to handle this issue. No one ever enjoyed responding to Darlene's calls. Her son Dicky was a hothead who always ended up in jail because he didn't like following directions. When he was drunk, it made every situation even worse.

He made it to their house within a few minutes since she didn't live far from the main drag. Dicky was pacing in the yard, holding a bottle of whiskey, chugging every few steps.

"The bitch had to call the cops, uh! If she'd just let me in so I could take a nap, it'd be all right."

"Dicky, your mother asked you to leave and sleep it off somewhere else. I'll drive you to Dwayne's house."

Dwayne was his brother, and if it wasn't Dicky causing problems, it was Dwayne. But when one was off their rocker, the other one was usually levelheaded. Dwayne would let Dicky in and sleep it off. He'd be able to handle him better than Darlene ever could. Neither had ever hit their mother, but they'd been known to throw and destroy stuff in the house.

"No." Then Dicky spit in his direction, missing his boots by a few inches.

Griffin had no desire to arrest Dicky because it would involve him resisting.

"If you don't leave on your own, you know where you'll be sleeping it off. Judge Riner is always busy on Mondays. He won't get to you until tomorrow. You and I both know how much you'll hate that."

Dicky slammed the bottle to his lips, draining the last of the whiskey. He tossed the bottle in Griffin's direction, forcing him to duck. That sealed the deal. He wouldn't be leaving without cuffs on his wrists.

"Turn around, Dicky, hands behind your back."

Instead of listening, which Griffin knew he wouldn't, he grabbed a plastic candy cane decoration from Darlene's garden and wielded it like a sword.

"Come make me." Then Dicky spit at him again, this time hitting the toe of his boot.

Griffin's mind veered back to this morning, lying in bed with Eve, kissing her and loving her so thoroughly she had whispered they should call out sick. He wished he'd given in to that simple request. Because then he wouldn't about to be in a battle with a drunken idiot.

A car drove by blaring music. "Jingle Bell Rock" of all tunes. But it motivated him to take a step forward and show Dicky he wasn't playing around today.

12

———

EVE PUT the last of the Danishes she made into the display, then stood up, flinching when Bob appeared on the other side of the counter. There was a short line. Theresa kept up a good pace helping customers. Yet he wasn't in line; he was standing in front of her.

"Hi, Eve."

She forced a grin out. The way he looked at her unnerved her for some reason. She saw him around town here and there, especially if she drove through any road work where he usually held the sign, directing traffic. He always made it a point to wave and smile at her.

"Hey, Bob."

He continued to stare at her with his creepy grin.

"Well, have a good day. I have to check on...the bread." Which was a lie because no bread was currently baking, and if they had bread in the oven, Chip normally took care of that.

"Always nice to see you."

She nodded, then turned, making sure to take slow, even steps to the kitchen. The last thing she needed was for him to think he bothered her, which he did. But she didn't need him to know that. Unable to help herself, she glanced behind her before stepping through the swinging doors. Bob was leaving, not getting in line to purchase something. Odd. Had he already eaten and decided to say hi when he saw her? Or had he just come in to say hi?

A shiver rippled across her body. She forced the weird thought out of her head. Bob could be strange at times, but he was harmless. Everyone in town had a bad habit of getting in a person's face. They couldn't help themselves.

The day crawled at a slow pace. By the time three rolled around, she was ready to go home. Since nothing had happened the prior week with Darrian, she'd told Griffin she felt comfortable enough to drive to work by herself. Her shift usually ended before his and she felt bad putting him out like that. Having to leave work to bring her home where she locked herself in the house until he got home himself. Simply silly when she could handle it on her own.

She'd seen the urge from him to argue with her about it this morning before they left—separately—but he conceded. Like he normally did. Giving her the space and the independence she craved. She loved his protectiveness, but she also needed to do this on her own. She had to prove to herself that she was capable of surviving without him. She didn't know what the future held. Though they didn't talk about it, leaving always sat in the recesses of her mind. She knew he knew it.

"I'll see you tomorrow, Jules." Eve grabbed her purse, slinging it over her neck.

Juliet popped her head up from some paperwork she was doodling with at her desk, tossing a wave her way. "You don't need to come in until eight tomorrow, if that's okay.

Theresa needs to leave early for a doctor's appointment. If you could close for me, I'd appreciate it."

"Of course. I don't mind."

Eve didn't ask if she'd be closing by herself. She could only assume so if Juliet needed her to come in later, which meant Juliet herself would be leaving before closing as well.

"I'll swing by the homeless shelter as well, drop off the leftovers."

Juliet frowned, waving her off. "It's fine. Don't worry about it."

Why could everyone else bring the food there and she couldn't? Juliet felt she was capable of closing the cafe on her own. Why did she think she wasn't capable of dropping off food at the homeless shelter?

"But I want to."

Juliet looked up from her papers, her frown increasing. Chip was already gone, having left thirty minutes earlier. Only the two of them were in the back. Not that she wouldn't have said anything in front of Chip, because she would've.

"Well, then I'll ask Griffin to accompany you." She went back to her paperwork.

"I'll do it on my own."

Juliet sighed. "I'd prefer you didn't."

Eve's hands tightened on the strap of her purse, slung across her chest. To the point she felt the leather dig into her skin.

"Why? Why don't you trust me?"

Juliet stood up with a pained expression. "It's not that I don't trust *you*."

Okay. The way she emphasized *you* meant it had to do with something else—someone else.

"Explain, please."

They stared at each other for the longest time. Juliet finally sighed, her shoulders slumping as if admitting defeat.

"Gerald, my ex-husband, his brother, Gregory, runs the place. I should've known from his brother alone that Gerald wasn't the man I thought he was. He's never pleasant to me. Ever. Not even when we were dating." Juliet drew her eyes to the ground. "I saw the way he looked at you the first time you helped me. I don't want him to do anything to you."

The place was always busy, full of people. Though there were times when delivering the food, they were the only ones in the kitchen. Juliet was afraid Gregory would corner Eve and force himself on her. She'd admit, she'd have a hard time fighting any man off. She never could fight off Darrian.

But what about Juliet? She went there on her own. She didn't worry about herself?

"You go alone."

Juliet nodded. "I try not to. But I also don't want that asshole to think he scares me, so I do on occasion. It's unfortunate he runs the place because I'd like to avoid him. He blames me for his brother in prison as if I did something wrong. If I don't have to put you in an awkward position, then I won't."

Eve bit her bottom lip, the nerves darting forth. She pushed them back. "I'd like to deliver the food on my own. I've no doubt he knows about my issues. I don't want him to think he can scare me either. If I don't want to think of myself as weak, then I need to prove it to myself. Do you think he'd be that stupid to put his hands on me?"

"I wouldn't say those two are the brightest bulb on the tree. Gerald always had a short temper, unable to control himself. Gregory could be the same. I didn't like how he looked at you."

Eve shrugged. "I'm used to people staring at me. That's all everyone always does in my life. Stare. Judge me. What's one more person?"

"Okay, fine. I don't like it, but I trust you to know what you want to do. I hate it when Griffin and Bryce try to do things to hold me back, and I won't do that to you. Call me when you leave the place."

"I can do that. Thank you. I appreciate your faith in me."

"Hey, if you change your mind and you don't feel comfortable doing it, that's okay too. I didn't go there by myself for a long time. I hate admitting he scares me, but he does."

"I'll be careful."

With the conversation over and settled, Eve said good-bye and left. The drive home was uneventful. She honestly didn't expect anything less.

She'd yet to get used to the alarm blaring in her ears before she managed to press the numbers to disarm it. It made her feel secure having it, especially with Griffin still at work. She plugged the numbers again, resetting the alarm.

After showering and changing into new clothes, she decided to start supper. Though when she looked through her fridge and pantry, nothing popped out and said, "Make me!" She settled on chicken and potatoes after much deliberation. The chicken defrosted in no time, then she added some seasoning to it. She peeled the potatoes, cutting them into small pieces and layering them around the chicken. She put the lid over the casserole dish and then shoved it into the oven. Then she cleaned up her mess, turning to the dish towel she had hanging on the wall to wipe her hands.

Her entire body froze.

Pink hearts splattered around a white towel stared at her.

That wasn't right.

She knew she had hung up a towel with red, white, and blue stars on it. It was almost August. Not that Labor Day was close yet, but from May to September, decorating the house with the American colors felt appropriate for the summer season. She would never have hung up hearts.

Would she have?

No. Definitely not. She distinctly remembered hanging up the other towel two days ago.

Maybe Griffin changed it on her without her knowing.

Okay. That sounded like a more plausible explanation than the one rolling through her mind—that someone else had entered her house and changed the towel. But why? And if it was Darrian, why do little annoying things like moving her stuff around or changing a towel? What was the end goal?

She jumped, screaming when the doorbell went off.

With her heart racing, she walked to the front door and peered through the peephole. Her entire body jolted back.

It wasn't Darrian on her doorstep, but the second worst thing to be standing there. His lawyer. A man who could cut through any red tape with nothing more than a rusty nail file.

A GROAN ESCAPED as he shifted in his seat, the pain in his back flaring. Griffin should've gone to the hospital like Duke suggested, but he was already running behind and he didn't like leaving Eve alone for too long.

It was nearing six o'clock and he should've been done by five. She'd been on her own for the past three hours. He'd busted his phone in the melee with Dicky, so he'd been unable to check in with her.

Juliet hadn't called the office and had dispatch reach out to him, so he assumed Eve left without any issues. No calls to nine-one-one, so he could also assume no issues when she got home. Still. He needed to see with his own eyes that she was okay. Just because a week passed with no word from her brother didn't mean nothing would happen.

He tensed when he pulled into his driveway, eyeing the man he didn't recognize on her doorstep.

The aches and pains running up and down his body grumbled as he threw open his door and stalked to her house.

"Can I help you?"

The man turned, eyeing him up and down. Yeah, he didn't look the best. His shirt had been ripped, so he'd changed into a T-shirt he kept in the trunk for times like this. He'd changed before he'd wiped all the blood off, so he smeared some on the shirt. He had the start of a black eye on the right side of his face, along with a bruised cheek. His left arm was covered in gauze where Dicky had swung the candy cane and cut him good. Not enough to warrant stitches, but enough that it bled.

"No, you cannot."

Then the man turned back toward the door, knocking. More like pounding, in his opinion. Griffin knew Eve was home because her car sat in the driveway. Since it'd been at least a minute, going on two since he pulled in and exited his vehicle, he knew she wasn't answering the door on purpose. This gentleman wasn't Darrian, but he could only assume he was someone Eve knew.

"She's not answering. So you can leave."

"You can mind your own business," the man snapped, glaring.

Griffin had his service weapon strapped to his waist. Didn't the man see it? Reasonably assume who he was speaking to? In case he didn't, Griffin swiped his badge from his back pocket, returning a glare with flare.

"It is my business. I'm telling you to leave this property."

The man stepped closer. "Do you know who I am?"

"Someone not welcome here." Griffin shoved his badge back into his pocket, resting his hand lightly on the butt of his gun. "But please, enlighten me with a name."

"Bryan Torrenson. I'm the attorney for Darrian Carrington. And I'm not leaving until I speak to Evelyn. We're worried about her safety."

"She's fine." Griffin narrowed his eyes. "Now that she's far away from her brother. She's perfectly fine."

The man's nostrils flared. "I'm sorry that you think Mr. Carrington would hurt his sister. He would never. I suppose you're the one who bullied her into filing that preposterous protection order."

"There's only one bully standing here, and it's not me."

"I would be careful with what you say. You have no idea who you're dealing with."

Wow. This jackass thought forceful words with a demonic glare were going to scare him. Not likely.

"And I don't think you understand who you're dealing with. I told you to leave, and if I have to say it again, I will arrest you for trespassing."

Bryan smirked. "Evelyn hasn't asked me to leave, and seeing as it's her property, your word means nothing."

"Well, seeing as she rents the property—from me," he emphasized, loving the way the guy's eyes rounded in surprise, "I'd say my word holds a lot of weight."

It appeared they were in a standoff now. Bryan continued to stare as if weighing his next move. The only move Griffin would allow was for him to leave the property.

The door swung open, causing both of them to turn toward the sound. Griffin could see the agitation in her stance, yet the bravery coating her eyes.

"You heard Chief Stuart. Leave the property now. I have nothing to say to you."

"Evelyn—"

"It's Ms. Carrington to you!" she snapped, cutting Bryan off.

"Your brother is concerned about your welfare. He'd like to speak to you."

Eve crossed her arms. "Well, he's not allowed to. I have nothing to say to him. Or you."

Griffin glared at the man as he walked past, taking a spot next to Eve. She was handling herself well, but he felt better being closer to her. Being a lawyer, he didn't think Bryan would be stupid enough to lay a hand on her. But one could never know what another person would do.

Bryan nodded. "I wish you felt differently. We will be contesting the order. We'll see you in court."

"Until then, you can stay away from Eve. If I see you on this property again, there will be no chatting. Just cuffs." Griffin's hand tightened on his weapon. He knew Bryan saw the gesture, though he made no comment on it.

He turned around and left without another word. As soon as he was nowhere in sight, Griffin looked at Eve, who gasped at him, finally noticing the bruises.

"What happened?"

"A tussle with an idiot today. I'm fine."

She brushed a tender hand across the red mark on his

cheek. "You look terrible." Then she pulled him inside, pointing to the couch. "I'll grab you some ice."

"I'd like to take a shower. My eye is fine."

Her arms wrapped around him, laying her head gently on his chest. "You keep saying that, but it doesn't look like it."

He lifted her head, cupping her cheeks, then pressed a light kiss to her lips. "Are you okay?"

She shivered but nodded.

"You didn't have to come outside. I would've handled it."

"And I was going to let you." A tentative smile emerged. "Then I remembered you telling me how strong I am. If you want me to confront Darrian, I need to practice with other nasty snakes first."

"You handled him beautifully." Griffin kissed her again, harder, more insistent. Her hands tightened around his waist, making him groan and wince in pain.

She released him, stepping back. "What am I going to find under your shirt?"

He gave her a wry grin. "Nothing pretty. It was a helluva fight."

"Come on." She grabbed his hand, pulling him toward the hallway. "Let's take that shower."

His lips widened so far, it hurt. "Together?"

"Someone has to take care of you."

She lifted his shirt gently, gasping at the bruises marring his chest. Then her lips touched his skin, making him shiver, but not from pain.

Their clothes disappeared. The water was hot and soothing. Her hands full of suds were even more soothing as she wove around his body, washing off the blood and grime from the day. Everywhere she touched lit his body on fire. So gentle. So tender. So full of love.

Neither had yet to say the words, though they teetered on his tongue every single day. When she touched him with such patience, he could only hope she loved him in return.

They kissed, they explored, but they kept it light and carefree. He didn't think his body could handle anything heavy and strong at the moment, even as his body ached to slam her against the wall and shove deep inside.

They dried each other off, then she pulled him to the bedroom where they lay down, curling into each other.

He brushed a few wet strands of hair off her cheek. "Thank you. I'm already feeling better."

Her brows puckered as her hands pressed against his chest, holding them there.

"Did you change the towel in the kitchen recently?"

Odd question.

"No, why?"

A tremble coated her body. "It's nothing."

He pulled her closer, as close as they could get, cocooning her in his warmth and safety. "Tell me."

Her eyes sparked with fear for the first time that night. Even outside when she confronted Bryan, she held more courage with a touch of anxiety, but not fear.

"I don't remember putting the towel with hearts out there. But nothing else looks out of place. The alarm was set when I got home." She shivered, then chuckled. "I probably did and forgot. I'm being silly."

"Trust your gut, Eve. If you didn't change it, then you didn't. I'll look into it tomorrow. We'll figure this out together." He kissed her forehead, vowing to himself that he'd figure it out or die trying.

A kiss hit his chest, then another. She wriggled out of his arms, pressing kisses along the way, until she hit his cock that was waiting for the ultimate kiss.

He touched her head, relishing in the desire he saw reflected in her eyes.

"You don't have to do this."

She licked her lips. "You're always making me feel good. Worrying about how I'm feeling. It's my turn to repay that sentiment. You lay back and relax. I'm going to take good care of you."

Then her mouth swallowed his cock, sucking and licking, and he could do nothing but do as she said—lay back and relax. For a small moment in time, nothing mattered but the pleasure zinging through his body. Not the aches and pains covering every inch of him. Not the problems making her life hell. Not the fact he feared he'd lose her one day—and not from her psycho brother.

She moved effortlessly. Her mouth and tongue did things that had him pumping his hips, needing more, wanting more, but also wanting it to last even longer. His hands touched her head, holding her in place, as if afraid she'd stop. Yet not tightly, not wanting her to think she had to continue. His low groans mingled with her sweet moans as she continued the assault on his cock. To the point he couldn't take it anymore.

"Sweetheart, I'm going to come. Oh, god." He grabbed her head to move her, yet her lips tightened around him, sucking even harder.

He groaned, his entire body taut with bliss as it spread throughout him. She sucked every last drop that spilled from him, then light, feather-like kisses trailed up his chest. Her head rested against him.

His hand wove up and down her back, his eyes closed, his body spent.

The words 'I love you' sat on his lips. He wanted to shout

it out. He wanted to hear it in return. He wanted to move her out of this house and into his.

Instead, he kissed the top of her head, then let the effects of the day take over, and fell asleep.

13

"Go on. I'll take care of this," Griffin said, kissing her lightly and forcing himself not to push her out of her own house.

Her foot tapped incessantly as they stood near the front door. "I should help."

He framed her face, staring into her gorgeous emerald eyes. Oh, how he wished they could rewind the morning to an hour earlier when she was curled in his embrace and he was loving her as if it would be the last time.

"I'm going to check the alarm out, do a bit of digging to see if anyone was inside the house. You don't need to be here for that. Juliet's expecting you. I got this. I don't want you to worry about anything."

"Maybe my mind is playing tricks on me and I did change the towel yesterday."

"And maybe you didn't." He dropped his hands, grasping hers. "It doesn't hurt to make sure. Now stop worrying and have a wonderful day at the cafe. I'll see you after work."

She hesitated, then nodded, kissing him before leaving. He watched her from the doorway as she pulled out of the driveway and disappeared from his view.

Griffin shut the door and searched the house, checking windows—something he'd done last night before they went to bed. He messed with the alarm, confident it was working correctly. Nothing seemed amiss with the security of the house. But someone had gotten in somehow. With Darrian's attorney in town, he was afraid of who the culprit was. Though why he'd mess with her towel was odd.

After calling the alarm company and finding out someone used the code to get inside the house in the late morning, his body went rigid with tension.

Damn it!

Someone had been in the house.

He didn't enter it and he knew Eve had been at work. No one else had the passcode to her house. Even if, say, Juliet had the code, she had no reason to enter Eve's house. Not even Stan, the guy who installed the alarm, knew the code.

Griffin stood near the door, looking around. How did the person get in? How did they know the code? If he changed the code, would they figure it out again? He was missing something. Something vital, and it irked him the answer wasn't glaring in his face.

Thirty minutes later, after going window to window, slower this time, he was nowhere closer to an answer than he was before.

A knock on the door stopped his intense thoughts.

Duke stood on the other side when he opened it.

"Sherry said you wouldn't be coming in today after the fight with Dicky yesterday. How are you feeling?"

"Better today." Thanks to a beautiful woman with soft, tender hands. "How'd you know where to find me?"

Duke's brows rose as if saying, "Seriously?" "You didn't answer the door when I knocked on your house. I figured I'd try Eve's first before leaving. I stopped in at the cafe. I heard about the"—he shrugged— "towel incident when she was chatting with Juliet. Find anything?"

"Not a damn thing. Stan looked up the records, and it shows someone punched in the code yesterday, late morning. So someone was in here. I can't figure out how they know the code. Eve picked the code, but the numbers mean nothing to her."

Duke propped a hand to his hip. "So the dick lawyer couldn't have guessed it?"

"I don't think so, but I'm not ruling him out. How'd you hear about him?"

Duke chuckled. "Well, he's staying at Mrs. Donahoe's B&B. That shit was known by suppertime last night." His smile fell. "I've been keeping an eye on the cafe. He hasn't stopped there yet."

Griffin's expression hardened. "And he damn well better not."

Duke looked at the door standing open behind Griffin. "Did you change the locks after the last tenant?"

He nodded. "Of course. But even if I hadn't, that doesn't account for the fact there wasn't an alarm then and how they could've figured out the code."

"Well, there are devices that can decode that shit." Duke tossed his head toward the door. "But there's no marks on the door to indicate it was pried open or anything. How about any other points of access?"

"It all looks clear. Shut tightly. No marks. No indication someone broke their way inside."

Duke pointed toward the outside of the house. "Maybe you need to put cameras up outside. Catch the culprit that way."

Griffin mused that for a moment. "Cameras?" Then he turned around to the living room, looking around again.

"This house was empty when Eve moved in. She's had the sense someone's been moving things around since the very start."

"So not the dick lawyer?"

"Why don't you grab a ladder from my garage? Let's do some more searching."

They found the first camera hidden in the light fixture in the living room. Great vantage point for someone to see Eve punch in the alarm code. No need for any special device or guessing the numbers. The person saw it. The second one was hidden in the kitchen vent in the ceiling. The camera found in the bedroom didn't disturb him as much as the one in the bathroom did. Sure, they had been very intimate in the bedroom, but spying on someone in the bathroom seemed more violating.

His mind ventured to what had transpired in the bathroom last night, washing each other so thoroughly. Then fast-forward to Eve and the way she devoured him with her mouth. How invading. To think someone had that on film disgusted him.

Well, it was over now. They'd found every camera and dismantled them. They stood in the kitchen, the devices sprawled across the table.

"You okay, Grif?"

He flinched, forgetting that Duke stood by him. A tight jerk of his head said he was, but he wasn't. No way in hell he'd tell Duke the things he and Eve had done, the sense of violation he was feeling.

"I need you to get all of this to the crime lab. I need to know who did this."

Because when he found the culprit, they were going to pay. He wasn't even sure he wouldn't throw a punch or two. Beat them to within an inch of their life. When Eve found out...it wouldn't compare to how he was feeling. She'd feel a hundred times more violated.

"I'll have them search every inch of every device to get a print."

"I want to know where these came from." He swiped a hand across his jaw. "It's going to be impossible to trace who purchased them or from where. Too easy to buy these things from the internet these days. I need something found on this shit."

"We will." Duke's tone was very confident.

Griffin didn't hold the same confidence. This person had been doing this since Eve moved in. Watching her. Spying on her. Making her think she was going crazy by moving things around the house. Breaking her safe space by entering her home.

The bastard would pay.

"While you do that, I'll change the locks." Again, which irritated him. But now that the person didn't have access to the house—because he'd change the code too—they shouldn't be able to get in again. And he'd add cameras outside as Duke originally suggested. If anyone approached the house, he'd know.

"You know, a lot of people moved in and out of this place the past year," Duke noted casually, though there was nothing simple about the words.

His jaw tightened. Damn it. He should've found this a long time ago.

"I'll call Mindy. Get contact information for everyone that lived here in the past year. See if they had anything odd happen to them."

Griffin nodded, appreciating Duke's help. Clearly, he wasn't capable of much at the moment, with the anger consuming him. "I want that list too. We'll split it up."

Despite the anger flowing through his veins, he wasn't about to let anyone else handle this on their own. This was his job, and he'd make the person regret ever stepping foot in this house.

FIVE O'CLOCK HAD PASSED. Juliet and Chip had already left. Theresa was cleaning up in front while Eve tidied the back. She wouldn't be baking anymore, so she'd have to go up front soon. When Theresa left, she'd be alone. Which was fine. The sun still shined brightly, and Main Street was always busy and full of people. There would be nothing to worry about.

Griffin hadn't popped in at all, which bothered her. But only because she wanted to know how the day went looking for answers. He'd sent a few texts checking in with her, but he didn't mention anything about her house, and she had been afraid to ask.

Maybe he found nothing. Maybe she was seeing things that weren't really there. She changed the dumb towel without remembering and that was that.

Theresa popped into the back. "Tables are cleared and clean. I rearranged the displays, though not much is left. No one is out there right now, but you know the few stragglers that come in right before closing." She grabbed her purse, a slight frown marring her face. "Do you want me to stay until closing?"

While she appreciated everyone's concern—since they all knew the lawyer was in town—she didn't want to be coddled. She could handle this. She *had* to handle this.

"I'm good. I'll see you tomorrow."

With no choice now, she waved good-bye to Theresa,

who left via the back door and went up front. As Theresa predicted, the few stragglers—some regulars, some tourists—stopped in and depleted most of the sandwiches. She even managed to finish the soup of the day—tomato bisque. There were a few Danishes and croissants left, along with some sweet treats that the shelter would appreciate tonight.

She had fifteen minutes left to go when the bell above the door jingled. Looking up from the display she had been messing with, her body froze.

"Ms. Carrington, finally, alone at last," Mr. Torrenson said with a wicked smile.

Darrian's lawyer was as smarmy as Darrian himself. She had never liked the way he looked at her, as if she were prime meat ready to devour. Though the man had never actually tried anything with her, she could be thankful for that.

"I have nothing to say to you. Please leave."

"You have no idea what you're doing." He stopped at the counter. "How long do you think you can play this little charade before you see the truth?"

The only truth she knew was if her brother got near her, he'd kill her. That's the only truth that mattered.

"If you're not going to purchase anything, you will have to leave." She tried to make herself sound confident and in control, but even she heard the tremble in her tone.

He laid a manilla folder on the counter. "We'll see you in court. You might think you're going to win, but you won't. Why don't you make things easier on yourself and return home with me?"

Over her dead body. Literally. She would never step foot out of town with this man.

"Get out."

He stared at her long and hard, not moving an inch. A

throat clearing behind him had his bravado jerking for a second, though he covered his surprise quickly. Turning, giving her a view of who stood behind him, had her heart slowing down its erratic pace. Duke stood with his hand on the butt of his gun and a fierce expression. She had expected Griffin to be standing there since he always seemed to come to her rescue, but she'd take Duke as well.

"She told you to leave. You step foot in this cafe again, you'll be arrested."

"It's a public establishment," Bryan spat.

"One that says you're not welcome, which would mean you're trespassing. The owner herself, Juliet, told the police department you're not welcome in here. This is your only warning. Next time I'll grab my cuffs without speaking."

"My business here is done." Bryan turned to her, striking her with an arrogant look. "I'll see you Friday."

Then he passed Duke as if he hadn't threatened to arrest him. Duke walked to the counter, his eyes filled with concern.

"You okay?"

She nodded, even though nothing was okay.

Duke's gaze trailed to the folder on the counter. "What's that, if you don't mind me asking?"

Eve shrugged. "Court papers or something." Her hand trembled as she picked it up. Part of her wanted to ask Duke to look, even though it wasn't his business.

Most of it held legal jargon that she was too wired up to decipher. But the bottom line: Darrian was contesting the order of protection. The court date on Friday would decide whether it would continue.

The good thing: it would occur here in town. On her turf.

The bad thing: Darrian would be in attendance. She had to face her brother.

"Judge Riner isn't going to side with him."

She looked up, realizing Duke had glanced at the papers as well. Not that she had tried to hide them from his prying eyes. What did it matter if he knew? She figured the whole town would know by the time she stepped out of the cafe because that's how this town operated. News traveled at the speed of light.

"He strikes me as a fair and partial man. He'll listen to Darrian's side of the story." Eve's voice lowered to a whisper. "Darrian has a lot of sway in a lot of places. Money speaks more than I care to admit."

Duke leaned closer, whispering himself. "And Judge Riner is a better man than that. You're safe here, Eve. I promise you that."

Her eyes lifted. "Thank you, Duke, for your support. I appreciate it."

His cheeks bloomed a light red as he pulled away. "You have a lot more support than just me." He looked around the cafe as if embarrassed for some reason. "The cafe closes in five minutes. I'll wait for you to close up and follow you home."

She waved him off. "I need to stop at the shelter first and drop off the food. But thank you."

"Not alone, you're not."

Her lips thinned in a tight line. "I've had this conversation with Juliet, and I'm going. I will be careful."

"I don't even like it when Juliet goes alone." The tightness in his jaw and the worry that glazed his eyes added to the venom in his tone.

"Duke...I need to do this by myself. I don't want to be afraid of things."

"Same thing Juliet says to me, and I don't like it when she says it either. Accepting help isn't the same as hiding behind someone else."

"I don't want to argue with you."

Which was odd they even were. Sure, she had light conversations with him when he came in for lunch on occasion. She waved to him when she saw him patrolling around town. But this level of honesty and closeness was new. She appreciated the concern, but this was something she wanted to do alone.

"Good. Then we'll go together."

She laughed despite the seriousness of it. "You're as stubborn as Griffin can be."

"Take that as a compliment, Duke. She must mean it as one," the man himself said, walking up behind her, sliding his arms around her waist, and kissing her neck.

He must've slipped in from the back. It was locked from the outside, but he had a key. Why had he come from that way and not the front? Did it matter when feeling his arms around her made her feel better? Safer.

"Well, I'll let you continue to argue with her. See you tomorrow, Eve. Looking forward to the cookies you bake." Then Duke left.

Eve twisted in his arms, kissing him. "What are you doing here? What did you find?"

She felt him tense, knowing he'd found something.

"I said this morning I'd see you after work. Well, it's 6:01 and it's officially after work."

Giggling, she pressed her head against his chest, tightening her arms around his waist. "I assumed once I got home."

"I can only guess what you and Duke were arguing about since I didn't hear the first part, but you're not going to the shelter alone. He's right. I don't like it when Juliet does it either. Today, don't fight me on it. Please."

She heard the worry, felt the fear. Whatever he had found today, she knew she wouldn't like it. For that reason alone, she chose not to argue.

"Do I want to know what you did today?"

His lips caressed her neck, his heavy sigh telling her everything. Then his words confirmed it. "Nothing good, sweetheart. Nothing I want to tell you. But I will."

He lifted her head, cupping her cheeks. "Because we're always going to be honest with each other, even when it's hard to do so."

Then he kissed her so fiercely, she wanted to forget about everything left to do for the night and drown in his embrace.

14

GRIFFIN DIDN'T SEE Gregory when they carried in the food leftover from the cafe. Cheryl was working in the back, greeting them with a smile. The entire encounter took no more than ten minutes, chatting with Cheryl most of the time. By the sly smirk on Eve's face, she was silently telling him she could've handled it. He had no doubt. But after today's findings, he needed to *feel* needed. To know he could protect her if need be.

Because for the entire time she'd been living in his rental, he'd failed to protect her.

Knowing someone had violated her privacy—their intimate moments—was too much to bear. His mind had roiled with agony all day as he tried to find answers.

He had also struggled with ways to tell her what he found. Nothing sounded good. How did you tell someone you found cameras all over their house? That they'd been spied on from the moment they stepped into the space?

He'd spoken with Mindy, who had been appalled by the news. Duke had spoken to her first, getting the information about the previous tenants, but Griffin had wanted to speak to her as well. She had nothing new to report. No idea who could have installed cameras in the house. That's what bothered Griffin the most. Who could have gotten access to the property to do such a thing? Sure, he hadn't had a security system until recently, but he had good locks on the windows and doors. It would've been hard to break in without making it noticeable, and he found no indication someone had done so.

The place had been used as a rental for the past two years. The first year went smoothly with a nice couple, who after the first year, decided to buy their own house in town. They had wanted to see if living in a town with Christmas cheer every day was something they'd like. They had. Since they had moved out, no one had lasted long.

Griffin had decided he'd follow up with them first while Duke tackled the other people. Of course, when he went by Scott and Erica's place, they weren't home. Scott worked at one of the two doctor's offices in town as a pediatrician. That's when he found out they were on vacation and wouldn't be back for another few days. It had disappointed him, but he hadn't sweated over it. He wasn't sure what they'd be able to tell him anyway.

He'd spent the rest of the day changing the locks and installing cameras outside the front and back doors. No one was getting inside without him knowing this time. He had it all hooked up to an app on his phone that would alert him of any approaching company.

They'd left Eve's car at the cafe. He'd bring her to work tomorrow, something he never minded doing. When he parked the car in his driveway, they sat there in silence for a few moments.

"I think—"

"What did—"

They stopped speaking, looking at each other. He could drown in the depths of her emerald eyes. Right now, they held a hint of fear, but also curiosity. She had been about to ask what he found out today. And he had almost stupidly ruined everything by suggesting she move in with him.

He knew better than that.

Pushing her too soon, too fast, and he knew she'd flee as far as she could. But the thought of her stepping into the cottage alone had him itching to make her stay in his house —forever.

Her lips twisted into an easy grin, though the fear still touched her eyes. "You go first."

"I think we should eat on the patio tonight. Have a glass of wine."

Her brows puckered. "Okay, maybe I should've gone first. What did you find? What aren't you telling me?"

Yeah, that was silly of him, thinking he could gloss over the subject and she would let it go. At least she didn't call him on his lie. That hadn't been what he originally wanted to say and she knew it.

He took a deep breath and let it out slowly. Then everything came out. From the moment he found the first camera to making sure each piece of equipment they found was searched with a fine-tooth comb. He wanted answers and he wanted them now!

She shivered, wrapping her arms around herself, her gaze turning from him to the cottage.

"I wasn't going crazy."

"I'm so sorry, Eve. I am so unbelievably sorry."

Her head whipped to him, her hand reaching across the seat to graze his cheek. "You have nothing to be sorry about."

He grasped her hand, setting it down between them, yet

didn't let go. "I should've known what was going on. It shouldn't have happened in the first place."

Keeping the venom out of his tone was impossible. By the way she flinched, he should've done a better job of hiding it.

"It's not your fault, Griffin. I don't know why you'd think it is."

"It's my house."

She unbuckled her belt, scooting closer, bringing her free hand to his face. "Always the protector. You know now, and I'm not worried. You make me feel safe. It's over now."

That's where she was wrong. It wouldn't be over until he found the culprit. He wouldn't sleep easy until that happened.

"Stay with me tonight." His grip on her hand tightened, forcing himself to keep the remainder of his plea inside. For her to stay forever in his domain.

"I'd like that."

She removed her hand from his cheek, tugging on her other hand for him to let go. Reluctantly, he did. They fell into their easy routine of making supper, eating and cleaning up as if they'd been doing it for years together. He walked with her to her house to grab a few things, pointing out after she insisted where the cameras had been.

He saw the trembles each time they crossed over her body. Though she made no other reaction.

They were back at his house in short time. A movie stretched the evening out, and when it was bedtime, he tried to erase the day from his mind by making sweet, slow love to her.

The alarm the next morning jolted too soon. Eve rolled out of bed first, taking a shower and making breakfast while he lagged behind. He didn't want to start a new day. He wanted to lounge in bed. Touch her. Soothe her. Himself some. Forget the world and the troubles in it.

When he pulled into the back alley behind the cafe, he wrapped his hand around her neck, pulling her closer.

His lips were soft when all he wanted to do was crash them upon hers. Release all the anguish, the frustration, and the love he held back. But knowing she needed slow and easy, he refrained from making a fool of himself.

"I..." *love you.* "Wish we could've stayed in bed all day long today."

She smiled against his lips. "Next time say something and we can play hooky."

He knew neither of them would've done it, but it was nice to pretend.

Then his hand tightened and his expression turned fierce. "Call me if you have any problems. And I mean anything."

She backed away as best as she could with his hand still wrapped around her neck, frowning. "Nothing's going to happen. I told you Darrian isn't stupid."

Yeah, and now they had an unknown entity to deal with as well. Someone who'd been breaking into her home since the moment she arrived. Griffin didn't know why or what this person had been doing, and having the unknown glaring at him wasn't something he enjoyed. It unnerved him.

"Doesn't mean I won't worry."

She pressed her lips against his as if that would dispel the unease in his stomach. It didn't, but he enjoyed her sweet touches anytime she bestowed them.

Then she was slipping out of the car, and he worried for some inexplicable reason that she was slipping from his life.

EVE FIGURED after finding the cameras and knowing she hadn't been going crazy that her anxiety would settle down. Instead, it was in full-blown panic mode. She sensed Griffin on edge, disappointed in himself he still had no answers. Three days had gone by since he located the cameras and nothing. Of course, rushing the process couldn't be done. As soon as forensics finished doing their job, hopefully, they'd have the answers they wanted.

On top of that, today was the day she'd see Darrian for the first time since she fled. She knew that was the reason for the majority of her anxiety. Just seeing his face.

Juliet had given her the day off despite her protests. She'd go to court and then go to work. But Juliet knew her better than she knew herself. Or the simple fact she'd been through this sort of thing herself. Once court was finished, she'd need a breather from everyone.

Even Griffin.

Of course, telling him that wouldn't go over well. He wouldn't understand. She knew Juliet would, but the thought of talking about it frightened her.

"You ready?" Griffin popped his head into the bathroom doorframe with a gentle smile.

She knew he was hiding his own worry behind the easy twist of his lips. Their worries were completely opposite though. She feared Darrian would get his way and the protection order would be null and void. Griffin worried about her and how she'd react to everything.

Her brush hit the counter with a soft thud as she nodded and returned a smile. It didn't reach her eyes, but if he could pretend then so could she. They walked out of the bathroom and toward the front door.

"I thought we'd have some lunch two towns over afterward. Rosetta's has some of the best Italian dishes in the area."

She strapped her purse over her shoulder, maintaining her smile. "Let's see how the day goes first."

Griffin brushed a hand across her cheek. "I won't let him hurt you. You don't even have to speak to him. Don't let him ruin your day."

Too late.

Darrian had ruined every day of her life. It was impossible not to let him ruin another one.

They left, arriving in town way earlier than they needed to. But better to be early than late. They swung by Mocha Merriment to grab a cup of coffee. No one said anything to her about the upcoming court appearance, but she could see it in their eyes they wanted to. Ugh. She still hadn't gotten used to that part of small-town life. Everyone knowing your business.

When they walked into the courthouse, she blinked in surprise seeing Juliet and Bryce standing in front of the doors that would lead to her fate.

"What are you two doing here?" She wished her voice sounded steadier. More in control of her emotions.

Juliet pierced her with a get-real expression. "We got your back. In everything. You're not alone in this, Eve." She stepped closer, lowering her voice. "I know how you feel because I've felt the same way."

Griffin and Bryce both exhaled sharply at the reminder of Juliet's past troubles, though both women ignored them as Juliet continued.

"He's going to try to make you feel insecure and small, like you're weak and pathetic. A glance here or a smirk there. Gerald did the same. Sometimes, it worked. I couldn't forget those moments of terror, and that one glance swept me right back to the moment. And then I'd look at Grif or Bryce and I felt safe. It reminded me I wasn't alone anymore."

"You never were," Griffin growled under his breath.

Both women still ignored it.

"I want you to have that same feeling. That you're not alone anymore. You have people right next to you, supporting you and loving you. That's why I'm here," Juliet said with a determined look in her eyes.

No matter what Eve might say—go away, I don't want you here—Juliet wouldn't listen. Eve appreciated the support more than she would ever be able to express.

Bryce tossed a thumb toward Juliet with a gentle smile. The same one Griffin wore earlier in the morning. "What she said, but better than I would've. Like I told you the other day, you're stuck with us."

That's something she didn't mind one bit.

Eve drew in a large breath, then let it out slowly. She turned toward Griffin and held out her hand. He was offering his support in every possible way, and she needed to make sure he understood how important that was to her.

The way his lips curled up into an easy smile as he slid his hand into hers said she'd conveyed the correct message.

They stepped into the courtroom, and Eve's heart lurched at the sight of Darrian. She managed to keep in perfect stride with Griffin and didn't bat an eye when Darrian twisted his gaze her way.

Eve smiled at Darcy, the sweet yet fierce barracuda when needed, who'd said yes in a heartbeat when Griffin asked to represent Eve today. Griffin kissed her before sitting in the front row with Juliet and Bryce, while Eve took a seat next to Darcy at the table to the right of the courtroom.

"You look very confident," Darcy said, leaning closer so Darrian wouldn't hear. "I know the nerves are swimming around, but you got this. Judge Riner is a fair man."

"Thank you for being here."

"Of course. Anytime you need me."

Despite the urge to look over at Darrian, she held it in. Nothing good would come from looking at him, other than the terror running rampant through her veins. As Juliet had said, the memories would assault her, and she didn't need that right now. Not ever.

Judge Riner entered soon after and the proceedings started. Darcy, who'd sat down with Eve two days ago, reiterated all the reasons the order of protection needed to remain in place. That Darrian was a danger to her and she didn't feel safe.

When Mr. Torrenson, Darrian's lawyer, started speaking, Eve felt her safety boat sinking. Not in shallow waters either. Deep, dark waters where she knew she'd perish.

"Your Honor, I have several documents that illustrate Ms. Carrington has been under severe mental strain in the past few years since her parents tragically passed away. Of course, it was also hard on Mr. Carrington. While he managed to contain those emotions, she struggled. In and out of treatment. Taking medication." He widened his eyes as if shocked by the news. "And sometimes taking said medication while under the influence. The police had to be called several times for her erratic behavior. If Mr. Carrington ever laid a hand on her it was to ensure she didn't harm herself. I also have several documents showing she has been admitted to the hospital at least three times for self-harm. Mr. Carrington wants nothing more than to make sure his sister is safe and cared for. He'd never harm her."

Eve's heart pounded so rapidly, she thought it would

burst right out of her chest. She watched in horror as the bailiff handed the papers Mr. Torrenson had given him to the judge. She knew without looking at them herself they would appear legit and legal. Because Darrian wasn't anything but efficient.

Lie. All lies, of course. But that wouldn't matter because he always won. She had fought back every single time he hurt her. And every single time, she had come out the loser. Today wouldn't be anything different.

The room was silent as the judge rifled through the papers. She stared straight ahead awaiting the verdict she knew was coming. She couldn't even turn around to look Griffin in the eye. Did he believe the lies too? Why wouldn't he? She'd lied from the first moment she met him.

Darcy, her lawyer, even tensed next to her as if also believing the words as the truth.

Judge Riner looked up, his eyes swiveling to her. She couldn't decipher what he was thinking.

"Mr. Carrington, what is your hope here today?" Judge Riner asked. "If I remove the order of protection, what are your intentions toward your sister?"

"Your Honor, before she ran away, I had spoken to her about being more active in the day-to-day operations concerning the hotels. It's a lot of work to run a business. I need more help. We're supposed to be doing it together. That's what our parents wanted. I want my sister to come home. I want to run the business together."

Bile coated her throat as his smarmy voice filled the room. She'd flee again before she ever went anywhere with him. The only thing he wanted was ultimate control. Over her. Over the business. Over everything.

Judge Riner met her gaze. "And Ms. Carrington, what are your thoughts on the company? You do own half of it. I can only imagine how difficult it is to manage. How do you intend to do that from here?"

All those reassurances that Judge Riner was an impartial and fair man felt empty. He wasn't on her side. He wasn't out to protect her.

"I've never had any say in the company. Every time I tried to tell Darrian I didn't approve of a change, he hit me. He made me sign whatever papers were in front of me. How am I to even help manage when I'm not allowed a voice to do so?"

Darrian remained silent, but Judge Riner darted a glance at him.

"So is your wish to help manage the company?"

Was it? She honestly never gave it much thought. Because what was the point when she knew she'd never get past Darrian?

But the last thing she wanted was for Darrian to get his way. To get full control of the company. He'd have to kill her first to do so.

"Yes, Your Honor. I'd like that very much. What I don't like is to be in the same room as Darrian or alone with him. Whatever you were handed are lies. With further digging and investigating each claim against me, the court would see the truth."

"Your Honor—"

"Mr. Carrington, I didn't ask you to speak," Judge Riner snapped.

Eve almost turned her head to see Darrian's reaction to being reprimanded but didn't. She'd lose all the courage she still had bottled up the moment she met his gaze.

"I will continue the order of protection until these allegations made against Ms. Carrington can be verified. I am, however, adding a stipulation that contact can be had between Ms. Carrington and Mr. Carrington concerning the business only *and* with both lawyers present. No other communication will be allowed. In two weeks, we will read-journ with the full facts and evidence before the court. An impartial company will look into the matter. Neither people on Mr. Carrington's side nor Ms. Carrington's side will be in charge. That is all."

Eve flinched when he hit his gavel, the loud boom filling the room.

Darcy let out a silent breath, then turned to her with a smile. "You did great."

"Doing what? Looking like a scared woman."

Darcy frowned.

"You believe those lies about me."

The frown Darcy wore turned into a fierce expression. The barracuda part of her was emerging. "When did I give that impression?"

"When you tensed next to me."

"I didn't expect it, but it doesn't mean I believe it."

Eve caught Darrian's gaze over Darcy's shoulder, shivering at the smirk coating his lips. He thought he had won. And perhaps he did. In two weeks, she'd find out.

Griffin blocked the rest of her view of Darrian as he walked out of the courtroom. She shifted away when he tried to touch her.

"Eve..."

"She thinks we believe the lies," Darcy said matter-of-factly as she pushed in her chair and slung the strap of her bag onto her shoulder and grabbed the folders from the table.

The hurt flashed in Griffin's eyes as his brows burrowed. "I don't believe a word that man says. I never would."

God, she knew that. She did. Yet the fear slithering

through her veins told her otherwise. Years of doubt and people turning their backs on her couldn't be erased in one moment.

"I'm sorry, Griffin." She swallowed hard. "Forgive me, Darcy."

Darcy sighed, offering a short smile, making her appear less frightening. Eve would never want to go up against her in a courtroom. "There's nothing to forgive. I understand. We'll keep repeating that we're on your side."

Darcy left first. She was surrounded by the Stuarts, and she didn't know what to say, or where to look. Because meeting their eyes was too much.

"I think I'd like to go home. Be by myself a little bit."

"I'll take you home," Juliet said before Griffin could argue with her. Eve saw it in his eyes he wanted to.

Juliet led her out of the courthouse; she didn't look back once to see more hurt in Griffin's eyes.

15

GRIFFIN SAT across from Bryce at Vinnie's Diner, waiting for their orders.

"What just happened?"

Bryce stopped fiddling with the napkin in front of him and looked up. "Same thing Juliet did when the trial against Gerald started. She needs time, Grif. That man is pure evil. You could see it in his eyes." Bryce leaned forward. "She's never had anyone behind her, supporting her. She needs time to fully accept that."

Griffin slumped on his side of the booth. "I want to be with her right now. I don't like this distance between us. I don't just mean in miles. There's this..." He spread his arms out and blew out a breath. "Emotional distance that I feel keeps stretching farther and farther, no matter what I do."

"I don't know what to say. I don't know how to bridge that. I can't even with Denise."

Griffin nearly rolled his eyes at that statement but stopped himself. In the beginning, Denise hadn't been so bad. They'd been happily in love. Over time, things deteriorated, and she turned into a monster. Griffin knew Bryce still loved her, otherwise he would've asked for a divorce.

"Do you think Juliet stayed with her? She hasn't even called." Griffin looked at his phone sitting on the table, wishing with all his heart it would ring.

"Look, I know you don't want to hear this, but it's best Juliet took her home. She knows what Eve's going through. What living with a monster is like."

It didn't make him feel any better.

"I love her, Bryce. I want her to move in with me. I want to build a life with her. Hell, kids even sound nice." Griffin shook his head in defeat. "And I know she's going to leave. I feel it in my bones."

"Have you told her any of this?"

"Hell, no. You think I want her leaving today?" Griffin took a drink of water to stop the nasty words that wanted to spew from his mouth at the thought of her leaving. "One wrong word, and she's gone. You heard her in the court-room. She wants to be part of the business. How can she logically do that from here?"

"People do it all the time, work from home. Sometimes, she might have to travel, but then you go with her. Have some fun in the sun." Bryce grinned, telling him how easy it could all be.

Question was, how did he convince Eve of that?

"Did you tell Judge Riner what you found out about the maid that died? What did he say about that?"

"He didn't say much. What is there to say? We don't have jurisdiction there. Cause of death was natural causes, according to the coroner. So he poisoned her with some-thing that made it look like a heart attack. She was twenty-seven years old. Too young to have a heart attack."

"Or the coroner lied on the report. We know this guy has his hands in too many pockets in that area."

"Well, again, no jurisdiction. Can't exactly get the body exhumed to have another autopsy done with accurate results this time."

Bryce ran a hand over his chin. "I have faith in Judge Riner. If he says a neutral party will investigate Darrian's wild claims, then we have to believe the truth will be revealed. We know those are lies. Even if Eve doubts that we believe that, we know the truth."

"I can't even be mad she doubts me. I get it. I really do."

"And that, my dear brother," Bryce replied, "is why she won't leave you. It might seem like it right now, but she's not going anywhere. I feel it in my gut."

His gut took that opportunity to speak, grumbling in agreement.

"See."

They both laughed, easing some of the tension that had been swirling like a tornado around them.

The food was great, as always. Griffin never doubted that. Not like the doubts that ticked away like a time bomb waiting to go off that Eve would leave him.

When they left the diner, Griffin wanted to go home and check on Eve. Bryce nixed the idea, urging him to let her have her space. He relented and headed to the office. Paperwork awaited him, not that he cared if it sat even longer.

The day dragged. Duke reported that Darrian and his lawyer had left town, which surprised Griffin. Leaving so soon. Though why not? Darrian thought he had won. That he would ultimately win in the end, even after an investigation was done. Griffin couldn't do anything about it, as Judge Riner meant neutral in every sense. Not even he could step in and help.

Well, good. He didn't want that man in his town or anywhere near Eve. She'd be happy to hear he'd left.

Or not.

Griffin wasn't sure he should bring it up. But honesty was important between them, so he'd tell her even if he didn't want to broach the subject.

When five o'clock finally rolled around, he was out the door on the dot. Enough keeping his distance. He needed to see Eve and make sure she was okay. If she wasn't, then he'd soothe her worries away in any manner he could.

Juliet's car was in Eve's driveway when he arrived home. So his sister had stayed the entire day. Did that mean Eve was stuck in a rut that she couldn't get out of?

He hesitated walking over to her house, then shook off the nerves, forcing the confidence out. If Juliet could be by her side, then there was no reason he couldn't be either.

His fist against the door was solid, and perhaps a bit too loud. He hadn't meant to bang on the door.

Eve opened it a few seconds later with a smile on her face and the worry erased from her eyes. It's as if she had never seen her brother earlier in the day and dealt a semi-blow to the bubble she lived in.

"I have chicken and broccoli in the oven. You're right on time." She left the door open for him to enter and walked back toward the kitchen where Juliet sat at the table snipping the ends of green beans.

"We went to the farmer's market today. There are fresh strawberries in the fridge if you want some," Juliet said in way of a greeting. It also gave him a clue as to why she was snipping beans in the first place.

"I can even make you a strawberry daiquiri if you'd like." Eve lifted a glass that looked like said drink she just offered.

"A beer is fine." He pressed a kiss to her cheek before walking to the fridge and grabbing his own.

He had expected to walk into...well, he wasn't sure, but not this. Smiles and laughter and like the day hadn't started with tension. His gaze caught his sister, who looked tired yet full of spirit. He knew he'd have to thank her in the best way for helping Eve today. For removing the terror from her eyes and making her forget what a horrible man her brother was.

"Duke stopped by," Juliet stated, throwing a cut bean into a bowl. "He said Darrian left town already."

Griffin nodded, darting a glance at Eve to gauge her reaction to the news she obviously already knew as she didn't flinch in the slightest. Then why say it at all because Juliet knew he'd have had to know. No doubt to let him know they knew and she was fine. Eve would be fine, no matter what.

"He thinks he won."

Griffin saw the slight tremble in Eve's hand as she cut an onion. Even her words were a bit wobbly. So not as unaffected as he thought. But she sure was putting on a great performance. For whose sake? His? Or Juliet's?

"The truth always wins." Griffin set his beer down without taking one sip and moved closer to her, boxing her in from behind. He wrapped his arms around her stomach and pressed his lips to her neck, lingering. "No matter what happens, I'm here. Always. I will never let anyone hurt you."

She sighed, leaning her back against his chest. She trusted him enough to know he'd always catch her.

"I know that. I'm starting to believe it. In all of you. Juliet has been..." She inhaled sharply, shivering as she let out the breath. "It's been a long day. I'm glad you're home."

"Me too." He pressed a few more kisses along her neck before forcing himself to stop. It wouldn't take much for him to have his wicked way with her. "How soon do you think we can kick Juliet out?"

Eve giggled, shimming until she twisted around in his arms. Her eyes were lit up with pleasure and gone was the anguish he had felt moments before. "Start helping with the beans and maybe we can make it faster."

"I'm on it." Then he snatched another kiss, winked, and grabbed his beer and sat across from Juliet.

"I hope we get green bean soup one of these days with all these you bought." Griffin made sure to add a charming smile to his wish.

"Juliet has offered to lend me her recipe, so you're in luck."

"But only if I'm invited as well," Juliet replied. "I am not missing out on some green bean soup."

"Deal!" Eve beamed with happiness at the prospect, and Griffin didn't have it in him to argue. Not when she looked so enamored at something so simple.

He'd do whatever he had to to keep that beautiful expression on her face.

EVEN THOUGH EVE knew the cameras were gone, she didn't feel comfortable yet in her own house. Again.

Why did it always come to that for her? Not feeling safe in her home.

While they had supper—a lovely one—at her house, when Griffin suggested sleeping at his house, she didn't argue. She even packed a bag because the thought of sleeping in her house sent the anxiety coursing through her.

Of course, she hid it as well as she could. Griffin was

already worried about her; she didn't want to add any more worries to his plate.

They had a restful night, despite the turmoil of the day, and the weekend went by just as pleasant. It helped they didn't venture from the house. Sure, Darrian had left town. She shouldn't be fearful of going anywhere and running into him. Not to mention Griffin would be with her, so it wasn't as if Darrian could hurt her. But it was the mere thought of seeing him that had her going into panic mode at the idea of leaving the house.

Griffin had sensed it, knowing her so well, and never once suggested going anywhere. Juliet and Bryce had spent the afternoon with them playing yard games while grilling as well. All in all, with a cloud of doom hanging over her head, the weekend went well.

Wednesday hit, and things were still going decent. No signs of Darrian or his lecherous lawyer in town, so Eve didn't worry herself into a stupor going to the front of the cafe for this or that reason.

Griffin showed up for lunch, and she had a tuna sandwich with him by the window, watching as people strolled by. Some townsfolk she knew, others were tourists looking way too merry, in her opinion. But it was fun to see them dressed up in Christmas cheer. She found it silly, but enough to put a smile on her face and see the brighter side of life. When most of the time her life was doom and gloom.

She set her sandwich down, wiping her mouth with a napkin, eyeing Griffin. He was unusually silent today. He'd greeted her with a kiss, but not as enthusiastic as he normally did. Which meant something was on his mind and he didn't want to share.

He met her gaze, a lopsided smile. "You're looking at me like you're about to start interrogating me."

She returned his smile with a mischievous one. "Well, you're acting like I need to. Where shall I start?"

He leaned forward, his lips widening into delight. The kind that would have her panties getting wetter than she'd like in public. "Anywhere you want to, sweetheart."

She drew closer until she was able to press her lips to his. The kiss was slow and sweet and bespoke of the promises for later.

"Talk to me. I know you're holding something back."

Griffin sighed, slumping into his chair. She didn't like how he retreated but understood why. She did the same thing when she didn't want to share.

"We found a print on one of the cameras we found in your house. I got the report before I came here."

She sat up straighter. That was not what she had expected to hear. The news wasn't something he enjoyed receiving, which was odd. He'd had a hard time holding in his rage since he found the devices.

"And?"

Clearly, she was going to have to pry it out of him.

"And it came back to Mark Wilson. Mindy's brother."

Another thing she hadn't expected.

"That could mean..."

By the fright in his eyes, he knew what she hadn't been able to finish. It meant that her house wasn't the only house with hidden cameras. Not when Mark had access to all the houses Mindy handled as a realtor. Mindy had said so herself that Mark was great about helping her out.

"Why are you eating lunch with me?"

Griffin's brows drew inward. "What do you mean? We had a date for lunch, and I would never cancel on you."

Eve stood up. "I'll get you a to-go box."

She didn't make it one foot away from the table before Griffin grabbed her arm and pulled her into his embrace.

"I don't want a to-go box."

"You haven't arrested him yet. You haven't spoken to Mindy. You haven't done anything about this yet because of me. So go do it."

His grip was gentle but impenetrable. If she wanted to fight to get out of his arms, he'd make it difficult. Problem was she didn't want to fight him. Not over something like this. But she knew he wanted to handle the problem, yet couldn't because he didn't want to hurt her feelings either. She would've understood if he had to cancel—for any reason. He should know her better than that.

"I haven't done anything about it yet because I'm waiting on Duke to get a warrant. Because when I find Mark, I'm not messing around. It has nothing to do with you. I swear."

"Moments ago you said you'd never cancel on me." Therefore, he wasn't taking care of it because of her. He didn't want to hurt her feelings in any way.

His cheeks brightened, caught in his lie. "Okay, I'll amend my words. I'd never cancel on you unless I absolutely had to. I didn't need to today. As soon as Duke calls, I will have to leave."

Which she understood, naturally.

"Were you not going to tell me? I had to interrogate you."

He chuckled. "I caved pretty quickly on that interrogation." His smile dimmed. "I didn't want to say anything until I had him in custody." He lowered his head until his lips touched her neck in a gentle caress. "Until I had the tapes from him."

The videos of all their intimate moments. She shivered thinking that disgusting pervert watched them in such a private act.

Griffin soothed her rattled nerves with another kiss.

"Don't keep things from me until you think I can handle it. Please," she whispered into his chest.

"It had nothing to do with whether or not you could handle it." Griffin swore under his breath. "You're one of the strongest women I know. You can handle anything. It was more something I needed to do for myself." He lifted his head, pressing his lips to her forehead. "I will tell you things right away from here on out, no matter my reservations about it. I promise."

She nodded, taking his word for it. Griffin expected promises to him be kept, then she knew without a doubt he'd keep the ones he delivered himself.

"Can we finish our lunch now?" He tossed his head toward the table where their half-eaten sandwiches lay waiting to be devoured.

"I've sort of lost my appetite."

His eyes glowed with understanding. Another reason he hadn't wanted to tell her in this moment.

"Do you think Mindy has any idea?"

His expression hardened. "I sure in the hell hope not. Because I'll arrest her ass as well."

Griffin's phone broke the moment, ringing sharply between them. He grabbed the device latched to his belt and answered it. The conversation was brief. Duke had the warrant.

"How about I make salmon tonight? I've been having a craving for it."

She nodded, not caring what they had for supper tonight. Who knew if she'd have her appetite back by then.

Griffin kissed her one last time, a deep, thorough kiss that told her not to worry and how much he'd take care of her. If she hadn't been mistaken, a touch of love that he had been unable to hide.

But it was okay. She'd soak up any love he was willing to give her.

Then he was gone.

She cleaned up their mess and went back to her work-table to make cookies. Sugar cookies shaped like snowmen and Santas.

As soon as she returned, Chip took his break. It was only her and Juliet in the back.

She relayed what she knew.

Juliet grabbed a rolling pin and started working on the dough Chip had set aside before his break.

Eve couldn't hold back the giggle as she watched Juliet attack the dough.

"What?" Juliet tried to look offended and failed. "Is it now a laughing matter?"

"Only when you look like you're trying to maim the dough."

It wasn't funny. None of it was, but laughter filled the room until they were nearly to the point of tears.

Eve spoke first.

"I have never felt more violated in my life, and that's saying something with some of the things my brother has done to me. I've been thinking some very violent thoughts against the person—Mark—this past week, and I shouldn't. He'll pay in the correct way. I have to find solace in that." A trembling breath released. "Thanks for laughing with me. I needed that. I'm starting to feel better."

"I'm always here for you, Eve. Always." Juliet raised the rolling pin. "In any way you need me."

Eve understood her meaning. She appreciated it more than she could express. But when it came down to it, she didn't want to lower herself to their standards. Mark's. Her brother's. Anyone who hurt someone else. That wasn't her and she never wanted it to be that way.

The song concerning the snowman lying in front of her blared through the speakers. She rolled her eyes at the annoyance of hearing the song for the fifth time that day.

Then started singing it.

Because why the hell not? She needed something else to help lift her spirits, and there was nothing like a bit of Christmas cheer to help.

16

"So..."

Griffin let Duke's one meaningful word sift through the air. That combined with his hand resting on his weapon as they walked toward the house told him everything he needed to know.

How were they going to handle this?

A little interrogation first? Find the tapes? Throw the handcuffs on and be a little rough? Griffin wasn't sure which approach to take, especially when the anger coursed through his veins.

"You take the lead," he said through clenched teeth. Because he didn't trust himself not to lash out at Mark. Though he wanted to beat him to within an inch of his life, he couldn't. He believed in the law—even when he was a victim himself—and touching one hair on Mark's head wouldn't be following the law.

Duke knocked firmly on the door. It took longer than Griffin liked for Mark to open it. Worry had filled him that Mark knew and fled, until his innocent face stared at him.

Easygoing smile. Relaxed posture. Friendly eyes. He had no idea they knew his crimes.

"Hey, guys. What's up? Is it time to talk about the Labor Day parade already?"

That wasn't an unusual question. Considering they just rolled into August, it was time to think about the parade coming up in a month. Only about two hours long, but the event shut down half the town and most of the roads in the area. Mark helped on some of the floats, building and organizing them.

Duke held up his hand, the warrant dangling in it. "We have a warrant to search your house, the garage, and the shed you rent on Mr. Gornerish's property. In addition to your arrest as well."

Mark's friendly facade evaporated in a blink of an eye. Griffin knew at that exact moment he was guilty. That the print they found wasn't a mistake. Because part of him had hoped it was some sort of error. A contamination in the lab or something. It had been ridiculous to contemplate for even a moment. But the thought of someone he'd shared jokes with, a beer or two, and even gone to his fortieth birthday last year was too much to handle.

"On what charges?" Mark demanded, his hand tensing on the doorframe as if preparing himself to run.

He wouldn't get far, but Griffin had no worries if he wanted to attempt it. He didn't mind tackling his ass and getting in a good punch or two. He'd be justified taking him down.

"We both know you know, Mark," Griffin snapped, "so cut the crap. Where is your equipment? Make it easy on us. On yourself."

Mark took a step back, and he and Duke tensed at the movement, until Mark swung his hand as if gesturing for them to enter. "Turn the place upside down. I have no idea what you're talking about."

Griffin didn't respond because he wasn't about to get into a useless argument when he knew the truth. Duke didn't have the patience for it either. He read Mark his rights and the charges against him, slapping on the cuffs with little fanfare. Griffin put on gloves to start searching the house, while Duke took Mark into custody.

By the time Duke returned, Griffin had covered the majority of the house, finding nothing.

"I'll check the garage."

Griffin nodded and continued in his quest in Mark's bedroom.

Still nothing when they were finished.

"There's the shed he rents."

Griffin shook his head. "I called Rafael to head there when you left. He hasn't found anything."

They stood in the living room, cushions on the floor, shelves cleared, and drawers removed. They made a good mess in every room, not caring in the least. Except they found nothing. One laptop and that was it. For the number of cameras found in Eve's cottage, Griffin knew Mark had to have a nice setup of equipment to monitor everything.

"There's a reason his print was found. We're missing something."

Griffin blew out a frustrated breath. Yeah, but what were they missing?

"Do you think Mindy is in on it? The judge might extend the warrant to her stuff."

It was a possibility Griffin had pondered but nixed in quick order. They were close for siblings, as he was with his own. But he honestly didn't think Mindy would stoop to something so low. Of course, he had thought the same about Mark as well, so his gut couldn't be trusted at the moment.

"Let's see what she has to say," Griffin finally said.

They found her at the realtor's office, chatting with a couple about renting a property on the outskirts of town. Mindy had one of the busiest jobs in town. Someone was always looking for a place to stay. Most wanted to buy and ended up renting because property was such a hot commodity in town.

Mindy was quiet after they delivered the blowing news of her brother's arrest. She sat rigid in her chair, and Griffin wouldn't say she looked guilty in the least as if she had known what her brother had been up to. She'd been in the dark as much as them.

"Do you have any idea where he'd store his equipment?" Griffin had to ask. He didn't expect an honest answer. In the end, Mark was her brother, and he knew she'd protect him. He'd do the same for his siblings, despite working for the law. When it came down to it, family was more important. Not that he'd ever have to worry about them breaking the law in such a manner. Maybe his feelings would change if they did do something heinous.

"There must be some mistake. Mark wouldn't...to think he'd..." She shook her head, the denial ringing clear. "You're wrong."

Griffin relaxed in his chair, tossing his foot over his knee as if he had all the time in the world. It was in complete contrast to how he actually felt. The anxiety was coursing through his body, revving to unleash a bout of anger the town had never seen from him before.

"I found multiple cameras in Eve's house. Too many cameras. His prints were on one of them. The only explanation for that is he put it there. Mindy, they were found in the bathroom and bedroom. Eve told me numerous times things had moved around in her house. He was breaking in and touching her things. He had access to the house through you. He has access to all the other properties you manage. Now, do you want to go down as an accomplice to all of this, or do you want to help us find his equipment? We don't have a warrant for your house. But we do have listed on the warrant for Mark that the properties he's helped you with be handed over. We will need that list, if nothing else."

Griffin let his words hang in the air.

Mindy, after a few minutes of silence, tapped a few keys on her computer before the printer went off. She swiped the papers from the device and flung them across the desk.

"Your list. Now get out."

Griffin gathered the papers, nodding. "You might want to get him a good lawyer. Because it is now my life's mission to make sure he never sees the outside of a prison."

They left without another word.

The list of properties she handed over was long. Too long. They'd never make it through it all in one day. But they decided to start at the top and make their way down and get as much done with the few hours they had left.

Griffin knew after the first house they visited it would take forever. The couple renting the house a few doors down from Eve were shocked and disgusted when they found cameras all over the house. The only solace Griffin could give them was the culprit was in custody. He couldn't give them any more than that until he found Mark's base of operation.

He didn't make it home until nine o'clock. He'd called Eve to let her know he'd be late. He figured he'd be crawling into her bed after a long, exhausting day. To his delightful surprise, he found her waiting in his bed. She'd made supper and prepared a plate waiting to be heated up for him. The food was delicious, the shower he took was quick, and the moment he pulled her into his arms, he knew everything would be okay.

Maybe it wasn't so farfetched to think she wouldn't leave. She'd had a choice to stay at her place and she chose him instead.

He fell asleep with good vibes flowing around him.

EVE TURNED ON THE RADIO, humming to the merry Christmas tune coming out of the speakers. To think, a few months ago she couldn't stand the holiday. Now she was turning on the station Sleighville had to purposefully listen to Christmas music. And she wasn't even at the cafe!

"Whoa. You're listening to something different." Griffin came up behind her, kissing her neck.

She bagged the sandwich she had finished making and tossed it into his lunch bag, then turned around in his arms.

"I'm feeling Christmassy today."

He cocked a brow. "On your day off?"

She couldn't hide the smirk brewing. "I'm not going into the cafe today, but I'm planning on doing some baking. I want to try something new, but I want you all to taste test it this weekend before I suggest Juliet sells it." She shrugged, turning her gaze to his chest, embarrassed to admit it. "I've gotten used to baking with holiday music in the background. I'm afraid I need it for my inspiration."

Griffin put a finger under her chin, gently raising her gaze back to his. "You can do anything you put your mind to. With or without Christmas music. I know for a fact that whatever you plan on concocting will be delicious. I can't wait to try it. What is it?"

"Not telling. Not yet." She twisted slightly, grabbed his lunch bag, and put it between them. "Have a good day at work."

He smiled, but it didn't reach his eyes. She knew why. He'd worked all day yesterday, going through the list of other properties, finding cameras in every one. Most officers were helping with it as it was a huge undertaking. It left little time to find where Mark kept his base of operations. The weasel wasn't talking. Asked for a lawyer and hadn't said a word since. But she knew Griffin was determined. He'd find everything and shut it all down. Remove all traces of people's privacy being violated.

Griffin took the lunch bag and then opened the fridge to grab an energy drink.

"I can swing by for lunch. We can eat together."

She swiveled back to the counter to clean up her mess. "No, you focus on what you need to do today. I'll be fine alone. I was planning on baking in your house, if that's okay. We stay over here more than mine, and you have more ingredients than I do."

Which wasn't a lie. But it also wasn't the full truth.

She didn't feel comfortable in her own house any longer. Not since those cameras were found. Griffin hadn't said a word of protest when he came home late Wednesday and found her in his bed. If anything, she felt in his embrace how much he loved it.

"Of course it's okay. You're always welcome here."

Then his warm breath was touching her neck again before his lips followed suit. What she wouldn't give to stay in his embrace all day. She knew that was impossible. He had too much work to do. Honestly, she wished she was going to work as well. Being a Friday, the cafe was always busy, but Juliet had suggested last night she take the day off. Probably because the townsfolk had been in her face again. A different reason this time—Mark and his disgusting behavior. As much as she didn't want to admit it, Juliet had been right. She needed time away from people. To process and come to terms with everything going on in her life.

So, she was going to take this day and relax. Well, in her mind, baking was relaxing.

"I should get going."

She turned around, kissing him soundly, needing that extra touch from him. He pulled her snug against him, telling her in that simple touch how much he wished the same as her.

Then he was gone and the house felt empty.

She set the alarm, feeling marginally better at being alone. Then got to work. She wanted to make several different kinds of truffles. Chocolate, sugar cookies, caramel. And they would all be Grinch style. Most people seemed to love the green guy. She was getting tired of red and blue lately, so she wanted to add another color to the mix. Since she never made any kind of truffles before, she wanted to practice first.

Music filled the kitchen. Wonderful aromas enriched her senses. A bout of peace entered her heart, making her even more grateful to Juliet for insisting she take the day off.

The first chocolate truffle she tried melted in her mouth. Absolutely divine. She could be biased though.

Lunch rolled around. A small salad with an apple did the trick to satisfy her. A short, yet sweet call from Griffin helped as well. Still no progress on his end—at least in the sense of finding Mark's equipment. They were almost done visiting all the properties, so there was that positive note.

By mid-afternoon, she was exhausted and feeling much better. On a more even keel. She cleaned up her mess, put her treats away, and took a shower. She had a few more hours before Griffin got off work. If he got off on time. Planning to relax on the couch for an hour or so before starting supper, she got dressed before heading for the living room. Her footsteps slowed as she eyed the front door.

The alarm was set, the door closed. Yet there was a manila envelope lying on the floor. A tiny corner of it was still underneath the door, suggesting they had shoved it underneath and not actually opened it.

But for a split second her heart hammered at the thought someone had broken in. In a sense, they still had. They'd broken her moment of peace. All that hard work this morning—gone. Poof!

Walter appeared, rubbing against her leg as if warning her not to pick it up. But she had to. She needed to know what was inside.

He rubbed against her again, meowing this time.

"It's okay, Walter. I promise."

She didn't believe her promise as her hands trembled picking up the envelope. She stood for a long time before finding the courage to open it. Nothing was written on the front. So it could be for Griffin and not her. Yet, she knew deep down whatever this was, it was meant for her.

As soon as her eyes hit the photos hidden inside, she knew her time was up.

He won.

Like he always did.

17

"As the mayor of the town, I feel like I need to release a statement. Assure all the folks that everyone is safe and the matter has been handled."

Griffin sat across from his brother in his office. Duke stood near the door, which was closed from prying ears.

They'd been at it all day, finishing the list of properties and finding cameras in every single place. Disgusting. His stomach gurgled with revulsion every time they found a new one. So many people. So many private moments violated. Only a sick bastard would do something like this, and Mark fit the bill. With his silence, it only made him even more heinous.

"Of course. Do what you have to do, Bryce."

Griffin meant it, yet by the annoyance in Bryce's eyes, he didn't believe him.

"So you don't want me to?"

"That is not what I said. I said the exact opposite."

"Do what you have to do," Bryce mimicked but with mockery. "The town deserves to know."

"And you can tell them what we know." Griffin sat

straighter. "The only thing you can't tell them is all evidence has been collected because we can't find the videos!"

Griffin pushed away from his desk, lowering his head and taking several long, deep breaths. The last thing he needed to be doing was blowing up at his brother. It wasn't his fault that they couldn't find any of the videos. Sure, they had the cameras, but those videos were still out there. Moments that weren't meant to be shared.

"We'll find them."

Duke's quiet confidence did nothing to dispel the anguish building a large hole inside him.

"I'm sorry, Grif. I get it."

Griffin lifted his head and shot his brother a dirty look. "I don't think you fully do. I don't say that to be an asshole, Bryce. But you can't understand it. There are things on those videos that..." He blew out a breath as he tore his gaze away. "I agree you should make a statement. Rumors will run rampant if you don't. It's better to be upfront about things."

"Grif—"

He threw a hand up to stop whatever Bryce wanted to say. "I don't want to talk about it." He knew in the way Bryce started to say his name that he wanted to delve into a topic that should never be brought up.

Bryce's lips drew into a tight line. "Like Juliet never wanted to talk about it?"

That wasn't fair.

But it also hit right on the truth.

Gerald had hurt his sister. Things he and Bryce would never know. That bothered him, knowing his sister had suffered and he had been clueless. But he was understanding more about why she didn't want to talk about any of it. It didn't mean he liked it. Or that Bryce liked it.

"He had cameras set up in the bedroom and bathroom. I

think you can infer on your own why it bothers me we can't find the videos."

Bryce nodded. "I know you're not being an asshole when you say I don't get it. Because you're right. I don't know what that must feel like. I don't know what it feels like to get hit either like Juliet went through." A tremble coated his body. "But I know what it feels like to be degraded and yelled at constantly. As if my very existence has put the world in turmoil."

Duke inhaled sharply at the confession.

Griffin stiffened, gritting his teeth. "You should leave her."

He had no idea Bryce's marriage had gotten this bad. To the point she made him feel the way he just expressed.

That was the thing about life—you never know what goes on behind closed doors. Look at the secret Mark had hidden for as long as he had.

"I should. You're right."

Griffin heard the unspoken but.

But he wasn't going to. The question was why? Honestly, Griffin had no idea how they'd gotten this far off the original conversation.

Since he had no clue how to respond, he didn't. Nor did Duke. Bryce didn't add anything else. Silence reigned.

As each second ticked by, the air grew thicker, more awkward. He felt a tiny distance emerge between him and his brother. Something that had never happened before.

He wasn't about to let it happen now.

"I'm here for whatever you decide. No matter what. But I will say, Juliet didn't deserve anything Gerald did, and neither do you."

Bryce gave a short nod and that was it.

"Make your statement. I'm not sure we should admit

about the videos not being found yet. I don't want to cause a panic."

Bryce stood up. "I agree. I will give reassurance all is well because I know it will be." Bryce looked at Duke, then back at him. "You might not have found the videos yet, but you will. Because you're a Stuart, and Stuarts never quit."

With that true statement, Bryce left.

"Let's look at his financials. Maybe he bought property we don't know about. Maybe he's paying someone else to use their property or something." Griffin ran a hand through his hair. "They have to be somewhere."

"Let's do it. I may not be a Stuart, but I don't quit either."

Griffin chuckled. "That's why you're the one helping me."

They got down to business getting the information they needed. Pouring through the many documents in front of them made his eyes blur. Nothing abnormal stuck out. Mindy wasn't going to help them, but maybe Mark's friends would have some insight.

Before they could reroute in that direction, the mayor's office called informing them of the press statement Bryce intended to do. He had called a special meeting in the town hall for it. All citizens of Sleighville were invited to attend. Of course, it would be beneficial for the chief of police to be there as well.

He stood off to the right of the podium behind Bryce as he made a calm and collective statement regarding the arrest of Mark and his alleged crimes. It irked Griffin to the bone when Bryce used the word alleged. The man was guilty. There was no doubt in his mind. Though he knew that wasn't how the court of law worked, and Bryce had to do his due diligence while speaking on the matter. Griffin could tell from the people who had attended that their anxiety levels reduced from the moment they had walked in. Bryce always had that special way with people. Using flowery words to instill a sense of peace when in reality it was a shitshow.

The room was filled to the brim, not an empty seat in the place. Griffin wasn't surprised. Over twenty properties had been affected by Mark. That made for a lot of angry, violated people. Neighbors, family, and friends angry and violated on their behalf as well.

He'd texted Eve about the meeting, inviting her to come if she wished, but she had declined. He understood that. He didn't want to be here either. As soon as this thing ended, he was going home. Going to decompress from the treacherous day with the woman he loved.

Once Bryce finished his speech, hands lifted in the audience. Too many questions and not all could be answered.

The anxiety rose again, wiping out all the hard work Bryce's words had accomplished.

It was going to be a long night.

EVE LOOKED AROUND EACH ROOM, wondering if she had forgotten anything. She hadn't packed much. Necessities that would come in handy. Things that would look normal for leaving on such short notice.

Nothing was normal though.

The clock on the wall said it was well past suppertime. Griffin could be home soon, or he'd be even longer. It didn't matter how long it took, she'd wait for him. She had made a promise, and she wouldn't break it. Even if it gutted her inside to wait.

Her car was loaded and ready to go. She had close to a

full tank, so she'd get a good distance before having to stop. Oh, and she wouldn't stop tonight. She'd drive as far as she could.

A knock on the front door startled her. She blew out a deep breath as she walked from the bedroom to the door, peering through the hole before disarming the alarm and opening the door to Griffin.

He stepped in, kissed her on the lips, then sighed. It wasn't a sigh that meant he knew what she was up to. It was one displaying how tired he looked. Here she was about to blow his world apart even more.

"I saw all the goodies on the counter. You were busy. It smelled delicious in there. I was surprised you weren't among the goodies. Are we staying at your house tonight?"

"No, not tonight."

His smile wavered. "Okay. Do I have to wait for Juliet and Bryce tomorrow to try anything sitting on the counter? I hope not."

She forced a smile out, hoping to ease the discomfort forming on his face. But nothing would ease the blow she was about to give. "No, you can have as many as you like whenever you want."

He frowned. "Are you okay?"

No, she wasn't. She didn't think she'd ever be okay again. He knew her so well, not that she was great about hiding her emotions. She sucked at it.

"I have to leave."

His frown turned into a puzzled expression. "A few more details would be nice. I'm not understanding."

Spit it out!

"It's time for me to leave. You asked that I keep a promise. That when I wanted to leave I let you know. This is me letting you know."

Griffin took a step back, shaking his head. "Why are you suddenly wanting to up and leave? Out of nowhere? What happened today?"

Nothing she planned to share with him. For his own safety. He wouldn't understand if she tried to tell him.

"My car is packed. I have what I need. I don't feel comfortable taking the things you let me use, so I'm leaving all of those things. I appreciate you letting me borrow them."

"No, you're not going to ignore me, Eve. I want to know what happened today."

She forced herself to remain calm, to not display the terrifying trembles that she knew wanted to escape. Griffin looked pissed. Tight lips. Narrow eyes. Rigid stance. She'd seen the look on Darrian too many times to count. The only difference now was she knew Griffin would never physically lash out. Vocally, well, a man could only hold in his patience for so long. She knew that. She didn't fault him for it either. She'd let him release the anger bubbling to the surface and not flinch while he did so.

"I baked. I contemplated. I've decided to leave."

Which was mostly true. Minus the part where she received the most devastating news.

"You can't leave," Griffin croaked as if he were on the verge of tears.

If he cried, she'd break down into a puddle.

"You would've let me leave weeks ago without fighting me about it. I'd appreciate the same sentiment here."

Her voice was cold and methodic. Nothing displayed the turmoil going on inside her. But she had to remain stoic or she'd lose all the bravery she mustered waiting for him to return home. It would've been easier to run while he was gone. No defending herself. No explaining why. No one standing in her way.

"Is it about the videos? I haven't found them yet, but I will. Duke and I will find them. I know the town meeting tonight wasn't something you expected, and I understand why you didn't show up. I didn't even want to be there. You don't have to leave. I don't—" He groaned, his voice hitching. "I don't want you to leave."

"This has nothing to do with the videos."

She had sworn to herself she wouldn't lie to him anymore. That was no lie.

But she also couldn't divulge some of the truths.

"I love you, Eve. I want to build a life with you. I want you to tell me the real reason you're leaving. Stop lying to me."

Her bottom lip betrayed her, trembling at his confession.

She wasn't lying. Everything she'd said up to this point was the truth.

But she'd never tell him the real reason for leaving.

Now her eyes were going to be the traitors, building up with tears. Letting him know how difficult this was. How she was holding back. She blinked a few times to push them away.

"I haven't lied to you. I don't owe you any explanations. I think, deep down, you knew I'd never stay. So let's not make this harder than it has to be."

A muscle bunched in his cheek, he clenched his jaw hard. His eyes went from shattered to furious in a split second.

"Okay."

Then he turned around, his shoulders taut, his steps solid, and walked out, closing the door behind him with a soft click.

She expected more than just okay. *Needed* more than a stupid okay.

Balling her hands into fists, she pressed her nails as hard as she could into her palms to stop herself from screaming. From crying in anguish at how unfair life could be.

He didn't fight for her. For them. She knew he wouldn't. Because he was an honest man. He had let her have her space, her freedom from the beginning. If she told him she wanted to leave, he would respect that.

It didn't make it any easier.

She took one last look around, set the alarm, and locked the door. She told herself not to look at his house as she backed out of the driveway, but she failed. He was nowhere in sight.

Maybe he thought she wouldn't do it. She didn't the other time.

Well, this was different.

She kept her eyes straight ahead as she drove out of town. Twenty minutes later, she had to pull over to the side of the road. The tears streaming down were impeding her vision. Sobs tore out of her. Then came the screams she held in for so long. She even hit the steering wheel a few times before cursing at the pain in her hands.

Night descended. She had no idea how long she sat on the side of the road waiting to calm down.

Her eyes glided to the manilla envelope on the seat. With shaky hands, she pulled the photos out again. Snapshots of Griffin, Juliet, and Bryce. Around town. In their house. Driving unaware someone had their eyes set on them. A yellow sticky note attached to one of Griffin.

Call me.

Two simple words full of too much meaning.

He didn't have to sign his name to announce who to call.

Eve knew immediately it was Darrian's work of art. The pictures on their own weren't suspicious. But the why of it worried her.

So she called him.

Like he knew she would.

It hadn't been a long conversation. Enough to get his point across.

If she didn't leave and come home, he'd kill them. Every single one. The pictures were proof he could get them at any time, anywhere, and they'd never know what hit them.

Eve knew her brother was capable of murder. The maid was proof. The many beatings he bestowed upon her, nearly taking her life once was more than enough to take his words as gospel.

While she feared for her life every day, she didn't want to fear for Griffin or his family. She wouldn't be responsible for another person's death. Especially not the people who'd made her feel like part of a family for once.

She knew if she told Griffin what Darrian had done, he would've made promises that he'd keep her safe. That no one would hurt them. That wasn't something he could keep. She wouldn't have him or Bryce or Juliet looking over their shoulders for the rest of their life. Not like she planned to.

Because she left. She kept her word to Darrian.

But he was very mistaken if he thought she'd run back home to him.

Maybe it was time to be the predator for once. Not the prey.

18

GRIFFIN SAT SLOUCHED on the couch while Juliet paced in front of his coffee table. Bryce sat in the recliner looking as relaxed as him when he knew neither of them were relaxed. Walter, who didn't normally sit in his lap, was curled up purring. As if he knew Griffin needed comfort.

"I don't get it. I don't understand why she'd leave. Why'd you let her leave?" Juliet shouted, throwing her hands up in the air. "Why?"

"I'm not going to try to keep someone where they don't want to be. Eve knew that. I've never tried to make her stay. And if she doesn't want to stay of her own free will, then she doesn't. I won't beg anyone to be with me."

Juliet paused, turning to him, the anguish he felt sparkling in her gaze. "You know something happened. She wouldn't leave on a whim for no reason."

He nodded, agreeing. What else could he say? He suspected the same thing. But he knew how stubborn Eve could be. If she wanted to leave in that moment, short of tying her up, nothing would've stopped her.

Part of him had also hoped she wouldn't actually go. She

hadn't the first time. Because he'd given her space and let her make her own choice. He thought doing the same thing as last time would've worked in his favor. He'd bet wrong, and now he was paying the price.

"Did Darrian contact her?" Bryce voiced the question they'd all been thinking but hadn't said yet since Griffin had called to tell them she left.

It'd been two hours since he watched her from his bay window drive away. No word from her. No hesitation.

"She didn't admit to that."

"Well, if he threatened her, she wouldn't." Juliet shook her head, her face contorting as if tears would emerge any minute. "A person just can't erase the fear. She's had no one in her corner all her life. She's been on her own, living a nightmare and surviving the only way she knows how."

Griffin straightened, which startled Walter, causing him to jump off the couch. "She has us now. She knows that."

"Grif, maybe he didn't threaten her. Maybe he threatened you. One way to silence someone, to make them do your bidding, is to threaten the one thing they care about. Trust me, I would know."

Every time Juliet spoke about her past with Gerald, he wanted to break into the prison and beat the living shit out of the man. He hated hearing these things. But he also needed to know them.

"What..." Bryce hesitated. "What kind of things did Gerald threaten?"

Juliet looked away from both of them, turning her attention to the big bay window. Darkness poured in, not helping the melancholy filling the space.

"You know he was good with chemicals. He loved doing crazy projects with his students, showing the many wonders of science." Juliet wrapped her arms around herself. "One time when I told him I was leaving, that I was going to tell Griffin everything, he warned me that would be a very bad idea. He said he'd hate for Griffin to have car trouble or house problems because I was being a whiny bitch." She turned around, staring hard at them. "He had a look in his eyes that frightened me even more than when he hit me. He didn't have to spell out what he would do to you, Grif. But I knew he'd do something terrible, and it would be all my fault that you got hurt."

Griffin snapped to his feet, rounding his coffee table so fast that Juliet flinched and took a step back. He stopped a foot away before wrapping his arms around her like he wanted to.

"Nothing that man did was ever your fault. Anything he would've tried to do to me or Bryce or anyone else would not have been your fault."

She released a heavy breath, taking a step toward him. "That doesn't mean I wouldn't think it. He knew that. His threats worked for a long time."

He couldn't resist any longer, pulling Juliet into his arms. She held on tight, accepting his comfort and providing him with some of his own.

"I want in on this," Bryce pouted next to them.

Griffin opened his arm, yanking him into the circle. The way Bryce had said it and the way Griffin had added him made Juliet giggle. Which had been the point—mostly. Griffin knew Bryce hadn't wanted to be left out. They were in it together. The hard nasty stuff as much as the joyful things that happened in life.

They broke apart, stepping back but not completely where they couldn't start another round of hugs.

"So you think Darrian threatened me somehow? That's why she left?"

Juliet shrugged. "It's a possibility. How did she seem this morning? I didn't see or talk to her at all. Only you would know if the thought of leaving was on her mind."

"She was excited to bake this morning. She intended for all of us to try out the goodies this weekend. Nothing gave me cause for concern."

"Then something spooked her. Most likely Darrian."

Griffin had to agree with Juliet. It made the most sense. While he hated that Eve left, he understood the reason behind it.

"Let me check my cameras from today. I set up the same thing on my house as I did the cottage." Griffin ran to his office, Juliet and Bryce tailing him.

They crowded around his computer as he pulled up the software and started looking at the footage. They finally found what they were looking for in the afternoon. A man, not anyone they recognized, though it was hard to tell as his face was covered by the brim of a hat, approached the front door. He didn't knock, but he did shove a folder underneath the door. Since Griffin didn't have cameras inside his house, they had no way of knowing what was in the folder.

"I'm assuming she didn't mention this mysterious envelope to you," Bryce said, the first to break the silence after a long time staring at the screen.

Griffin shook his head and stood up from the chair, moving to the other side of the room. "What do we think was in it?"

"Something that scared her enough to run," Juliet said simply.

Yes, that much he knew.

"There's no way of identifying who that was," Griffin ground out, shoving a hand toward the screen. "You can't even see his face. He didn't park in the driveway, so he most likely parked farther down the street. No plates to run. We have nothing to go on, and I doubt if I try calling Eve, she'll answer."

"Well, I'll try then." Juliet pulled her phone out, groaning in frustration when Eve didn't answer.

They all tensed when the doorbell went off. Griffin rushed out of the room, swinging the door open, hope filling him up. He deflated when he saw Duke standing on the other side.

"I feel like I should apologize," Duke said with a chuckle.

"Sorry, man," Griffin sighed, waving him inside. "It's been a shitty night."

"Yeah, I know. Eve left." Duke nodded to Juliet and Bryce, who had entered the room, his eyes lingering on Juliet a moment longer than usual.

"How do you know that? Did you see her leave town? Which direction did she go?" Griffin tensed, waiting with bated breath for Duke to tell him something even better, like he saw her recently drive back into town.

"I received a call from Judge Riner not too long ago. He told me."

Griffin's brows puckered, not sure if this would be good news. "What's going on, Duke? Spit it out."

"Eve received some photos this afternoon. Of the three of you. Doing mundane things. Someone's been following you all. There was one little note on it saying call me. Eve knew it was from Darrian, so she called him. He told her if she didn't come home, he'd kill all of you. The photos were proof it could be done easily and without anyone knowing. She didn't doubt him for a second."

"I knew it," Juliet said, pointing at Griffin. "I told you. He threatened the one thing she wouldn't be able to ignore. Not just you, but all three of us because we welcomed her into our family and we threaten Darrian and what he wants."

"How does Judge Riner know all of this?" Bryce asked.

Duke smiled and that hope Griffin had yearned for earlier started to emerge once again. "She called Judge Riner from the side of the road and asked if she could see him. She showed him the photos and told him what Darrian said. That she was on her way out of town, planning to hide somewhere else, somewhere he'd never find her. But she changed her mind, she wanted to fight back. She told him she knew he might not believe her, but if he did, that she'd appreciate his help in the matter." Duke shifted on his feet, his smile increasing. "Well, we all know Judge Riner is a fair and kind man. Of course, he believed her. He has from the beginning, despite the lies Darrian spouted in court. Eve is on her way to Florida—"

"What the hell!" Griffin shouted. "Why in the hell is she going back to him?"

Duke gestured for Griffin to calm down. "Let me finish and I'll tell you."

Juliet put a hand on his shoulder, offering him support, but also a warning to let Duke continue. It was difficult to remain quiet when all he wanted to do was scream from the top of his lungs how much he wanted to hurt a judge. Why would he inform her to go to Florida? He had to because Eve had originally planned to flee and hide once again.

"He had a private investigator, a retired cop, and also a friend, handle the investigation into the claims Darrian stated in court about Eve. So far, based on what his friend, Ivan, has completed, nothing is turning out to be true, which we all knew it wouldn't. Darrian is the liar, not Eve. He told Eve to go to Ivan, who would help her. They plan to set up Darrian, catch him in the act."

Griffin tensed, grinding his teeth together. Even though Juliet put pressure on his shoulder, nothing would stop him if he suddenly rushed out of the house.

"What do you mean catch him in the act?" Griffin asked through clenched teeth. "Because if it's what I think you're suggesting, there's no way in hell that's happening."

"The only way to stop a monster is to trap it and take it down." Duke's eyes glided to Juliet then away before continuing. "This was Eve's idea. She knows what she's doing. She just needed some outside help."

"I would've helped her," Griffin whispered, the fight dying inside of him.

"She's protecting you." Juliet squeezed her hand before removing it from his shoulder. "As hard as it's going to be for you, you have to let her do this her way. We can't always have someone else fight our problems. In order to move on, we need to do this for ourselves."

"I hate that you're speaking from experience," Griffin muttered.

"But I am, which is why you need to trust me. Eve has got this. She's a strong, smart woman. And when she's done taking down this monster, she'll come back."

"And if she doesn't?"

Which was what Griffin feared the most. Either Darrian would finish the job or she'd decide this small town—him —wasn't what she wanted.

"She loves you, you idiot. Of course, she's coming back."

Well, it was better to believe his sister's words than the fear slithering around inside trying to take permanent residence.

❄

IT TOOK Eve two days to get to Florida. Though she could've caught a plane instead of driving, she didn't want it to appear as if she were eager to get here. Surprisingly, she was. The plan hatched, if it all went well, would end her nightmare.

Going to Judge Riner had been risky. She hadn't known if he'd believe her, if he'd be on her side. In the end, when she left his house, she realized he'd always been on her side. From the very beginning.

She crashed for a full day before seeing Ivan. Driving nonstop with a few breaks here and there, she needed a full day to recover. She'd need all her wits about her to get this done.

When she let Ivan into her hotel room, she had one moment where she worried she'd made the wrong decision. He had a stern expression, bushy eyebrows, and a physique that said he could crush her with one blow. But the kindness in his eyes and the gentle tone of his voice when he intro-duced himself washed away each worry. He had a slight accent that suggested he was from another country, confirmed when he spoke fondly of his home country, Ukraine. She appreciated hearing about him, sharing a few details about herself, making small chat before getting down to business.

"Don't worry, Eve. You are a strong woman. I know. I've seen many in my life, so I know when I am in the presence of one."

Slowly, she was starting to believe that herself. She wouldn't be back in Florida if she didn't think so at least a little bit.

"Have you finished all of your investigation yet?"

Judge Riner hadn't shared a whole lot, but enough to figure out that Darrian's lies were surfacing.

"Very soon. I haven't found a shred of what he has said to be true." Ivan pulled a metal bracelet with a few gems lined along the piece out of his briefcase. "When you wear this later today, we will hear more truths."

She slipped on the decoration. It fit snuggly against her wrist. It was very pretty. Gleaming silver with emerald and blue topaz stones. She assumed one of the stones hid the wired device. It looked real but not suspicious.

"He might not do or say anything right away."

At least, that's what she feared. As if Darrian knew her plans and would do everything in his power to thwart them. He always said he was smarter than her, than everyone. Now he could prove it.

"I'm here for as long as it takes. You're not alone." Ivan pointed to his ear. "I'll be listening the whole time. I won't be far away either if you need me."

Well, if Darrian lashed out, she'd need him. She'd yet to be able to fight him off and win. Why would this time be any different?

"Do I need to do anything?" she asked as she adjusted the bracelet, though it fit well so it was more of an anxious movement than anything.

"No. It's all set to go. You got this."

She had her doubts, but there was no turning back. When she drove through the gates of the mansion Darrian lived in, she knew she was stuck. At least until she took him down.

He opened the door before she even took one step toward it from her car. She couldn't determine whether that was because someone had been following her all the way from Minnesota—and if that were the case she was screwed —or if he had simply seen her drive up from the cameras at the front gate.

"You're home, Evelyn. I'm so glad to have you back. I do hope we can put our past behind us and move on. As a family."

His smarmy smile did nothing to ease the worries swimming in her gut. Though for prying eyes and ears, she returned a smile as if she agreed.

"Leave your stuff. The staff will unpack it. Let's have a drink."

She stiffened when he threw an arm around her in a friendly gesture, but she didn't try to remove it. She wouldn't have witnesses saying she wasn't showing kindness in the beginning. Everything had to go down with him attacking her for no reason. Which wouldn't be a problem. He'd done it so many times before.

They settled into the parlor with Darrian pouring them both a glass of wine. It wasn't even lunch, but she wouldn't refuse it. The glass would help with her nerves.

They made idle chit-chat as if they hadn't been to court a week earlier with an order of protection between them.

"I know you still need to settle in, but tomorrow, at the very least, we should talk business."

The hard glint in his eyes said he'd be doing all the talking, she'd be listening only.

"Of course. I can't wait to have a more active role."

He merely smiled.

Darrian excused himself, stating a meeting would need his attention for the remainder of the afternoon. Eve went to her room, not surprised to see her belongings already there. There wasn't much to unpack, and though it pained her, she hung up her clothes as if she planned to stay.

The day moved slowly with her sitting on pins and needles waiting for Darrian to corner her somewhere. Do what he always did.

But, like she suspected, he was on his best behavior. Supper was pleasant, and she feigned tiredness after, retreating to her room. She debated for a second whether to lock her bedroom door, resisting the urge. She wouldn't sleep well anyway. The sooner he tried something, the sooner she could leave.

Except, nothing happened. The next day, they drove to the office together where a board meeting was held. Business as usual. This time, she had a voice. She was able to offer suggestions without retaliation.

This went on for a full week. For the first time in her life, she lived in a home with pleasant conversation and normal smiles. She went to work, feeling like a part of the company for once. And Darrian was a gentleman through it all. She was waiting for the moment when he would lash out, and he wasn't giving it to her.

Was this her new hell? Living, waiting, pining for her freedom and he would never give it to her.

After almost two weeks away from Griffin, as she sat in bed, holding her phone, telling herself not to call him, she feared this was Darrian's plan.

To make her sweat. To make her wait. To make her wonder and worry when it would all go back to the nightmare she used to live in.

19

The knock on the door had him looking up from the paperwork sprawled on his desk. The distraction was needed. He hadn't been doing anything productive anyway.

Juliet smiled as she closed the door and took a seat across from him.

"You look terrible."

Griffin wouldn't disagree. He showered and put clean clothes on, but he hadn't shaved in two weeks, so he had more than just stubble growing. He ran his hand through his hair so many times throughout the day that it looked as if he hadn't combed it in weeks.

Two long weeks of not seeing Eve. No call. No text. No sign that Darrian intended to hurt her. Which he knew was bound to happen sooner or later. Once a monster, always a monster.

"Are you looking for me to disagree?"

"I'd like to say talk to me, but..." Juliet shrugged. "I get why you don't want to. I don't like it either about certain things. She's safe. We're safe."

Until Darrian put another hitman to watch them.

As soon as they learned about the photos, they went on the hunt. It was a small town. The people banded together when needed. Everyone might be in everyone's business, but they also knew when to keep silent but their eyes and ears open. They found the man—same hat from the surveillance camera in front of the house—staying a town over. Luckily for them, he had a warrant for his arrest. Not shocking, for murder. Because that's what hit men did.

So for now, no one was watching over them. Maybe because Eve hadn't left Darrian's side, so he didn't plan to send another one their way. The guy hired to watch them wasn't talking. Claimed he was there on vacation for some Christmas cheer. When questioned why he shoved a folder under the chief of police's door, he denied doing so. They knew the truth. So they couldn't get Darrian on any charges concerning that.

As for Eve being safe, Griffin didn't see it that way. She lived with a man who had beaten her too many times. One wrong move and he could hit her again.

Every night when he got home, he stared at his phone, wanting to call her. Every night, he went to bed proud of himself for resisting. Yet, he tossed and turned, finding no peace in that decision.

"I didn't come here to talk about Eve though."

He rolled his hand for her to get to the point. In the past two weeks, he hadn't hollered or lost his temper with anyone. He managed to keep the anger boiling inside right there. Inside. But it didn't mean he wasn't short and sometimes curt to people. His siblings included. They knew not to test the boundaries with him. Not right now. Not yet.

"I was watching a movie last night. Action thriller. It was intense." Juliet leaned forward, the glee rising in her gaze as if she were about to invite him over to watch it because it was that good. "Do you want to know the best part of it?"

He didn't have the energy to guess. By the look he gave her, she knew that.

"When the professor was browsing the books on the shelves, he pulled one and it opened a secret door."

She was sitting so far on the edge of her seat, Griffin sensed she wanted to jump across the desk to grab his shirt so he could see the excitement in her eyes even closer.

"Grif!" She slammed her hand on his desk, making him flinch. "Put two and two together."

He had no idea what she was talking about. If it wasn't about Eve...then what?

She sighed, rolling her eyes. "The tapes that you've been looking for. Maybe Mark has a secret room in his house. Which is why you only found one little laptop when we know he has way more than that."

He slowly sat up, letting the idea bloom inside. "A secret room? Like in an action movie?"

"Yes, like that." She rolled her eyes again for added measure. "When you set up cameras in that many properties, you're going to hide the evidence like you're a damn spy."

"Well, okay, then." Griffin stood up, grabbing his jacket from the coat rack in the corner of his office. "Care to help me look?"

Juliet bounced to her feet, rubbing her hands with merriment. "I thought you'd never ask."

Mark was still sitting in jail on the charges filed against him. The judge had set his bail to one hundred thousand dollars, and while Mindy tried to bail him out, she didn't have enough money to do so. Griffin found it noble she stood by her brother's side. Noble but stupid. The man was guilty, and she was only making herself more of an outcast in town. Nobody would talk to her or do business with her.

They made it to Mark's house in record time. Griffin had called Duke to join them. He pulled up at the same time they did. Mark didn't have a full library like the one Juliet had seen in the movie, but he had two shelves of books in his office that were prime pickings to be a lever. But when they moved each book, the wall didn't magically swing open.

Juliet rubbed her chin, then winced. "It should've worked. There should be a hidden room."

"It wasn't a bad idea," Duke noted. "But maybe we're looking at it all wrong. The book thing is common. It's in so many movies. I bet if Mark did build a room, he'd make it less conspicuous."

"Let's get looking." Then Griffin moved to another room.

After searching the living room, bedroom, and basement, they finally found the room they'd been looking for. The entrance was behind the pantry wall. If they hadn't been looking specifically for it, they would've never found it.

The room wasn't large, but big enough to hold four computer monitors and the rest of the equipment to do his dirty work.

Of course, his computer was password protected, but as soon as they cracked it and got in, Griffin knew he'd find all the video files that Mark had. The bastard was officially going down. And everyone, himself included, would have peace those videos were safe—and soon to be destroyed.

Duke took over, getting the crime lab to retrieve the equipment. Griffin drove Juliet back to town.

He parked in front of the cafe, planning to go back to Mark's house to help with everything.

"You know I'm here for you if you need me. We don't have to talk. We can watch a movie or something."

Griffin's hands tightened on the wheel. "I appreciate the support, Juliet. I'm not ready for that."

He needed his space at the moment.

"I know. I, of all people, know. Just as you respected my space when I needed it, I'll do the same. I wanted to remind you that I'm here."

He swiveled his gaze toward her. "That means the world to me."

Juliet exited the car, and he went back to Mark's. For the first time in two weeks when he arrived home, he didn't feel as much pressure weighing him down. They still had to crack the passcode, but it wouldn't be long. He had faith in that.

On the Eve front, his worries still burned a hole in his gut. Every day, he lost a little more hope that she'd return.

He took a shower, wiping off the grime from the day. Being in Mark's house had made him feel disgusting. He wiped the steam off the mirror, throwing the towel to the ground. The longer he stared at the man before him, the more he couldn't recognize who it was.

It took a long time to shave. One, because it felt so foreign to him after such a long time. He'd never tried growing a beard, so it was a new feeling. Two, because his hand trembled at times, so many conflicting emotions bombarding him.

When it was all over and he stared at himself again, clean and fresh, he felt a part of his old self return.

Right before he flicked off the lights to go to bed, he held his phone a moment longer than the other nights. Staring hard at the screen.

For the first time, he lost the will to remain strong.

EVE CURLED UNDER THE COVERS, gazing out the window at the moonlight filtering in. Middle of August and the heat suffocated a person when you stepped outside. She hadn't left the house today, but she'd stolen a few moments outside to get away from the stifling oppression she felt in the house. That had felt a hundred times worse than the heat outside. She ached to step out on the veranda and feel it again. Because the way she felt now couldn't be any worse.

Her phone buzzed on the nightstand, lighting up the tiny space.

She picked it up, gasping at the name and the simple words attached below it.

> I just wanted you to know I understand. And nothing has changed for me. I love you. I always will.

Oh, Griffin. How she loved him in return. His words meant everything. The despair that had been building slowly over the past week splintered, part of it breaking off and away. She had needed this. Though not his sweet voice whispering it to her, she heard it just the same as if he had.

Darrian could play this game forever. She could live in this hell until the day she died. Playing it safe wasn't working. She had miscalculated Darrian's strength to remain in check. She'd even felt Ivan wavering on Darrian's intentions. Though he continued to monitor and follow her around. Something she deeply appreciated. She didn't feel as alone and afraid because of it.

Her fingers hovered to reply when she heard a soft knock on her door. Twisting around, she saw a shadow as the door opened. She clutched the phone as it opened farther.

"Evelyn?"

She shivered at Darrian's low tone. It didn't sound menacing, but he never came to her room. Why now? Why so late?

She sat up, turning on her lamp on the nightstand, then pasted on the smile she'd been wearing since she returned home.

"Is something wrong?"

He shook his head. "I was hoping we could talk."

"Sure."

To her horror, he came inside, closing the door. She would've preferred he kept it open, but it was too late to protest. To be on an even keel with him, she slid out of bed and put on her robe. She wore a T-shirt and loose pants, but she still felt naked in front of him. With the robe, at least, she felt she wore some sort of armor.

Her gaze darted around the room, wondering where she'd put the bracelet. She'd taken a shower before coming to bed. A quick glance didn't help her, and she couldn't remember if she mistakenly left it in the bathroom. The bathroom wasn't far, the door open, so if she had she could only hope the bracelet would pick up anything he said from that far away.

"It's been nice having you back, having you at the office."

"I've enjoyed being there." She missed baking though. It was her true passion.

She missed the cafe. The dumb Christmas music blaring out of the speakers. The people not minding their own business, asking about personal things she had no idea they knew. That small town had been more than her refuge from danger, it had become her home.

She wanted to go back home.

"How long are we going to play this game?"

There he was. The monster she knew he could be.

"I don't know what you're talking about."

He smiled. Not his fake, icky smile that made her stomach gurgle with unease. No, the one that said he wanted to hurt her so badly she'd feel it for a week.

"Oh, you know, the one where you pretend like you enjoy being back, and the one where I pretend that I don't want to kill you."

She jerked at the venom in his tone but didn't make another move. She had nowhere to go. He stood in front of her only escape. The bathroom had no other adjoining door to get out of. She was three stories high. Jumping from the balcony would break her legs at the very least. Kill her, at the very worst.

"So we're at an impasse."

The maniacal laughter that left his mouth made her jump.

"Oh, Evelyn. No, I'm done pretending, so that means you have to go. You didn't think I'd let you live if you came home, did you?"

This time, she displayed her own smarmy smile. "Of course not, Darrian. You didn't think I came back without a plan, did you?"

That had him pausing, eyeing her in a new light. "And what is this plan of yours?"

She crossed her arms, tsking at him like a child. "You tell me yours, and I'll tell you mine."

Which wasn't possible because she had no plan. Her bracelet was nowhere in sight, she had no weapon to defend herself, and Ivan had no idea she needed help. She was a sitting duck.

But the last thing she intended to do was let any of that be known.

Darrian swiped his hand behind his back, producing a gun. "You're going to kill yourself. So distraught leaving the man you loved, you couldn't take it anymore. Your history of unstable behavior will back up the claim."

Ha! Ivan had disputed all those claims with his investigation. Judge Riner had all the evidence. No one would believe it. At least no one in her corner would.

"How are you going to shoot me so far away? That's not how suicides work."

"Well, you're not going to fight me, Evelyn. You never do. Not enough to win, anyway. Sit on the bed."

He waved the gun in her direction.

She could ignore his demand and make him shoot her, but she'd still be dead, and he may or may not get off with an explanation of why he shot her. Or she could comply and...and die anyway. Either way, she was screwed.

Except her phone was on the bed and she could call Ivan. It might not be enough time to save her, but it would be enough to put Darrian away for life, which had been the plan all along.

She moved to the bed, sitting down in a way that put the phone out of his eyesight. "So I'm willingly letting you kill me then?"

"Yes, Evelyn. It's easier if you don't fight. Because I can make it painful for you."

"Then I'd like to say a prayer first." She bowed her head as if doing so, saying a mini one in her head as she fiddled with her phone that he hopefully couldn't see.

Her head popped up when she felt the shadow hover above her. Darrian stood close enough she could feel the evil emanating from him.

"Why are doing this, Darrian? Why do you want to kill me?"

"Because you're nothing to me. Because you're in my way and nothing but an irritating gnat I need to get rid of."

"I'm sorry you hate me so much."

"Oh, Evelyn, I don't hate you. That would require emotion on my part. I care nothing for you."

"So what? You shove the gun in my mouth and make me pull the trigger?"

He laughed. "Oh, I'm not shooting you. Is that what you thought?" He swooped in so fast, she felt the needle before she saw it. He leaned in closer, his breath touching her skin. "You're going take a bath, to relax. Something you enjoy doing. Then you're going to slit your wrists. That's how you die."

She felt her muscles going weightless as if she were floating. Her mind fuzzy, yet aware. She feared whatever he'd dosed her with would make it impossible to move but feel everything. That's how horrifying her brother could be.

"Thank you, Darrian," she mumbled, nearly losing the ability to speak.

He cocked his head, frowning. "For what?"

"For telling me everything. So it's all clear." She inhaled sharply, hoping she had one more moment to speak. "Tell Grif...I love him...Iv...a..n."

"Oh, Evelyn. I'm sure your little cop friend doesn't even think about you."

She felt herself being lifted, yet couldn't move. Her arms dangled, her head lolling as Darrian carried her to the bathroom. She saw the bracelet sitting by the sink. No doubt, it heard nothing from the bedroom. Her only hope now was Ivan had answered and heard enough to have Darrian arrested.

Revulsion filled her as he set her in the tub, removing her clothes with little care to how rough he was. She felt every jab and jolt as he jostled her around. All she could do was stare at him, screaming inside her head.

Darrian had been right. She never fought back. This time she hadn't either. Not even one little punch. She'd complied with every word, and she'd die for it.

He turned on the hot water, scalding her skin. The cold tap remained off. Sick bastard! When he removed the knife, the fear intensified. She was going to die. She could do nothing but lay limp as he picked up her right wrist.

"No, I should do the left first. Then the right, where it lobs over the side and the knife falls to the ground." A horrid giggle filled the air like he was comedian of the year.

He reached over the tub, grabbing her other wrist. The knife touched her skin. Then the calm, booming voice that entered the room made her sing with joy.

"Step away from her or I will shoot you in the back."

Darrian jumped to his feet, swiveling toward Ivan, who stood behind him, his gun raised and level. He looked like he was bored and had nothing else to do. The only telltale sign that he was focused and ready for anything was the muscle bunching in his neck as if all his restraint was waiting to be unloaded.

"I found her like this. I had to pull the knife out of her hand. My sister..." Darrian's voice cracked as if distraught. "She's trying to kill herself."

Ivan nodded. "Yep, except for the part where I heard everything. She called me. Plus, you know, listening devices and stuff. It helps to have evidence when putting murderous assholes like you behind bars. Again, step away from her or I'll shoot you in the chest now."

Eve couldn't even warn Ivan that Darrian had a gun,

though she had no idea where it was. She couldn't recall if he set it down or put it back in his waistband. Only the knife dangled from his hand.

To her surprise, he complied, stepping away, tossing the knife to the floor.

"You have it all wrong. She—"

"I'll have to stop you there. I don't care to hear you speak anymore." Then Ivan moved closer and cold-clocked Darrian in the head. Ivan looked at her as Darrian slumped to the floor. "Bastard had it coming."

Ivan pulled a set of handcuffs out and locked up Darrian before coming to the tub to shut off the water, gasping when he stuck his hand in to unplug the tub. "That shit is hot. You're not moving or speaking so I can only assume he dosed you with something. Don't worry. I'll get you to the hospital."

Ivan grabbed a towel, averting his eyes as the water drained. When it was all gone, he covered her, then picked her up, carrying her to the room.

"An ambulance is on the way, along with the police. I promise you, you're safe now. I said I wouldn't let anything happen to you and I didn't."

Maybe her eyes spoke of how close it had gotten. Too close. Because Ivan chuckled. "Nothing like a little suspense to keep the heart pumping." Then he winked.

If she could've laughed, she would've. Because despite the seriousness of it all, his words made her feel lighter and on top of the world. As if she could defeat anything, at any time.

Because she just did.

20

SHE CURLED into the blanket as if that would hide her from everyone. Not that there were many people in the room. One nurse and Ivan, who stood near her bed waiting for the nurse to finish doing whatever she was doing with the monitors hooked up to her.

They had inserted an IV, which she felt every painful moment. The nurse hadn't been gentle. Stuck her twice before getting it in correctly. There was a device positioned on her finger and the blood pressure cuff wrapped around her bicep. She'd take it all though because it meant she was alive and safe.

Whatever Darrian had dosed her with had started to wear off. She could move, but slowly. Her entire body still felt weighed down, like she was stuck at the bottom of the ocean and couldn't move no matter how hard she tried.

After what seemed like forever, the nurse finally exited the room. Her gaze sought Ivan's, who wore a gentle smile as he took a seat in the chair next to her bed.

"How are you feeling?"

"Like I was hit by a massive truck."

Ivan leaned forward as if he wanted to reach out and comfort her somehow, but he settled for another encouraging smile. "You're safe now. Darrian will not be getting out. I made some calls. He's being booked as we speak, and the judge who will set his bail is not one who appreciates violent men. He'll get no bail, I know it. We have enough to make sure he is found guilty for attempted murder."

"But he'll eventually get out since he didn't actually kill me."

"We'll see. I've had a busy week. Protecting you. Getting the maid, who he *murdered*, her body exhumed. We'll nail him for that too."

"You're my hero."

In so many ways.

"Na." Ivan sat back, relaxing his foot over his knee. "You saved yourself. You did all the hard work."

Her eyes rounded. "I was in a bathtub naked, laying there for him to slit my wrists."

"But you managed to call me. You walked into that house knowing how dangerous it would be. That took a lot of courage. He wouldn't be sitting in jail if you hadn't had the guts to do that."

"You got to my room fast."

"Well," Ivan drawled, wincing with a short smile, "I'm proud of you for calling me. I heard every word and my testimony will help. But I'm not sure I would've made it in time with just your phone call."

Eve groaned as she sat up, hating how much her body ached from the slight movement. "What do you mean?"

"I heard muffling sounds. Like you were talking to someone. I couldn't make it out much. I saw the bracelet in the bathroom so I can only assume that's why I had trouble hearing things. It worried me that I couldn't hear anything.

You've been great about keeping it close to you. I decided to check on you. I was halfway inside the house when you called me."

Her breath hitched, realizing the implications. "You would've never gotten to me in time if you hadn't trusted your instincts."

He nodded with a grim expression. "But I did trust my instincts. And I caught him in the act. He had the knife in his hand. The tox report will show you were drugged. We have the needle that will likely have his prints and DNA on it. He's not getting away with it. I promise you that."

In the end, that's all that mattered. That Darrian went away and she could live in peace for once.

Where she belonged.

"I want to go home, Ivan. Get me out of here."

He stood up. "Of course. You sure you want to go back to that house?"

She shook her head. "No, I mean, my home. Sleighville. That's where I belong. Not here. Can I stay at your place until tomorrow morning when I can get a flight?" She sighed. "Or not. I can get a hotel room as well. I don't want to be a bother any longer."

Ivan stepped closer to the bed, squeezing her hand gently. "You have never been a bother. And you're more than welcome to stay at my place. But I will remind you that you own a private jet. You could leave right away if that's what you wished to do."

"A private jet?"

He laughed, stepping away from the bed and rounding it to get closer to the door. "It's not just Darrian's. Everything he owns and uses, so do you."

"Right. A private jet." It wasn't something that would cross her mind because she never liked being in the same vicinity as Darrian, so she rarely utilized it. "I would like to leave tonight. I don't know who to call to get that set up."

That showed how much she tried to ignore the life she'd grown up in. As soon as she returned to Sleighville, it could all go away for all she cared.

"Leave it to me. I'll have you out of here in an hour and on that plane." He grinned. "Well, maybe two hours. Let's see how fast I can work my magic."

And magic that man possessed.

She was released and sitting on her plane within an hour and a half. Between the timeframe he'd predicted. The flight took a little over three hours. When she landed, a car was waiting for her to drive her home. By the time the car pulled into the driveway of her cottage, it was a little past four in the morning. Exhaustion filled every bone in her body. She could sleep for a week, she was so tired.

But she thanked the driver and bid him farewell as she stood in the driveway staring at her cottage and then looking at Griffin's house. It didn't take much thought of which house she'd venture to.

She had a key in her purse to unlock the door but settled for ringing the doorbell instead. He'd texted that evening that he loved her and always would, but she didn't feel comfortable opening the door and letting herself in. Especially not so early in the morning. He might think it was an intruder and shoot her.

When Griffin opened the door, the dam broke. All the emotions she'd held inside from getting into the ambulance to sitting in the hospital bed to being curled up in the plane seat, it let loose. Sobs tore out. Griffin didn't say a word as he scooped her into his arms, closed the door, and went straight for his room.

He sat down on his bed with her cradled in his arms, letting her cry, soaking his shirt in the process.

GRIFFIN DIDN'T KNOW what had happened, but something had since Eve was on his doorstep so early in the morning.

Had it been his text to her last night? Making her see he'd always love her no matter what. That she could come home and all would be put in the past.

Or had something else more sinister happened?

He couldn't tell and by the sobs that ripped from her body, he couldn't ask her. Not yet.

Time passed slowly as he held her, rubbing her back. He wanted to whisper soothing words to her, yet refrained. He didn't want to say the wrong thing.

The tears gradually calmed and stopped altogether. Still, he kept silent, waiting for her to say the first word. He honestly didn't know what to say.

"I used a private jet I apparently own to get here tonight."

Well, that explained one thing. It also painted a picture of how far apart they were. How unattainable she could be if he let himself worry about that kind of stuff.

But she was here. That had to count for something.

"That's pretty cool. No waiting in those long airport lines."

She giggled, lifting her head as she wiped her eyes. "It was nice to skip those lines."

He wanted to kiss her. He wanted to pull her closer and wipe away the pain in her eyes.

"I got your text tonight. Did you mean it?"

His hand caressed her cheek. "Every word. I never

wanted you to leave. And when I found out the reason why you left, I wanted to go after you. I wanted to stop you."

"And yet you didn't."

"Because I knew you could handle it. Because I knew it was something you had to do. It doesn't mean I liked it. I had hoped you would come back after it all." His heart pounded as the next words rolled off his tongue. "Did something happen? Is that why you're back?"

She nodded, the tears building in her eyes once again. "I almost died tonight. By my own stupidity. By not fighting back. The only solace I had in the moment was that he wouldn't get away with it. That at least he'd go to prison for killing me."

Tears streamed down her face as she recounted the entire evening. Every word made him want to cry with her, yet he forced the emotions back, needing to soothe her. He nearly lost her tonight. He couldn't wrap his mind around it. The possibility that this moment could've been taken away from them.

"You're here now. You're safe."

So much had happened on his end as well, but the time didn't feel right to tell her any of it.

"I'm sorry for leaving."

"Don't be. You promised you'd tell me when you wanted to leave and you held that promise. I have no need to be mad about it. I get it. Like I said in the text. I understand."

He wanted to ask if her coming back meant she intended to stay. For good. But he couldn't seem to get the words out.

She sat up again, wiping more wetness away from her eyes. "So it's probably silly to keep renting the cottage."

His heart went from pounding steadily to an erratic pattern at her words. What did that mean? He was too afraid to hope what he wanted it to mean.

"Griffin?"

"I don't...I'm hoping that means what I think it does. I'm afraid to ask."

She smiled, brushing his cheek in a gentle caress. "Is it too presumptuous to invite myself to move in here? I'm at your place more than mine anyway."

"You're welcome to stay forever. Never move out." He pressed his lips hard against hers. "Ever. Marry me, Eve? Make a home with me. A family, if that's what you want."

"I've never thought about kids. Maybe."

His lips turned up into a wide grin. "And the marriage part?" Oh shit. He was rushing it. "Or moving in is a good place to start. Forget I—"

"Yes." She kissed him this time, hungrily and with the passion he'd missed the past few weeks. "I will not forget you asked, so don't even think about saying it. Yes, to it all. The entire time I was away, all I wanted was to come home. This is my home. *You're* my home, Griffin."

To think he never thought he'd hear that from her lips. Always worried she'd leave. Always on edge that it would all come crumbling down.

They celebrated with another deep kiss that led to clothes disappearing and their bodies joining as close as two people could get. Afterward, she fell into a deep sleep, something he knew she severely needed. She'd been through a huge ordeal. Rest would help her. Him as well. He hadn't been sleeping great since she left. For the first time in a long time, he slept like a rock.

He woke up first, glancing at his phone, noting it was already noon. He'd sent a text to his secretary before falling asleep he wouldn't be in the office today and if anyone needed him, they'd have to wait. He knew she'd relay the message to everyone who asked, which would be quite a few people. It wasn't very often he called out of work and with no explanation for why.

Eve looked peaceful, the color in her cheeks brighter than they were when he opened the door. He'd let her sleep longer. Sliding out of bed was easy as she barely moved, zonked out from everything. A quick shower awakened him even more, and the first cup of coffee helped the rest of the tiredness to evaporate. Though lunchtime, he opted to make breakfast.

Maybe it was the smell of bacon that woke her up or the fact he left the bed, but two warm hands wrapped around his stomach and pressed tightly.

Her lips hit his neck and he wanted more. He twisted around so he could see her, kissing her lightly on the mouth.

"Good morning."

She smiled, her eyes filled with happiness. So much better than the pain he had witnessed last night.

"Morning. I'm starving, and that smells divine."

"It's almost done."

"Do I have time for a shower?"

He nodded. "If it's quick. Another ten minutes for the bacon."

"I don't need a long one."

Then she was gone, and he wanted to follow her. Perhaps part of him still worried he'd lose her. She'd slip away if he didn't keep his eye on her. But he wouldn't become that person. That man who had no control of his emotions.

He stayed in the kitchen preparing the rest of the meal and timed it perfectly, pouring her a cup of coffee as she walked in looking more refreshed than before.

"I didn't pack any clothes. I hopped in the plane and

left."

He eyed her up and down, loving how she looked in his shirt and no pants on.

"You did leave some clothes in my closet. Though I like the outfit you picked out."

She lifted his shirt near her chest, inhaling. "I missed you. I need to feel as close as I can to you right now."

He wrapped her in his arms. "You can wear my clothes anytime you want." She shivered, bringing back the worry. "What's wrong? If we're moving too fast—"

"Stop. We had that conversation. It's not fast. I'm happy."

"I can tell something is wrong."

Her eyes dropped as she bit her bottom lip. "Is Juliet mad I left without saying good-bye? I didn't even give her notice at the cafe. That was very rude of me."

"Hey," Griffin whispered, lifting her gaze back up to his. "She is not mad at you. She's been as worried as me. If anyone understands what you went through, it's her. She'll be excited to hear you're back. So no more worrying about that."

"Okay. I trust you."

And he knew that didn't come easy to her. He'd cherish her trust every single day.

Breakfast was delicious. He took that moment to tell her everything that had occurred while she'd been gone. Finding the secret room and all the evidence that would put Mark away for a long time. Also how they had found the hit man and there was nothing to worry about anymore. When they were done eating, Eve told him to call Juliet and Bryce and tell them that she had returned. They didn't waste any time coming over. Bryce hugged her like a brother should— with love and affection. Juliet held on longer, giving her the reassurance she had needed that she wasn't angry with her.

"It's so good to have you back," Juliet said as they all settled into the living room. "Of course, take a few days off. When you're ready to come back to work, we'll be ready to eat your goodies." Then her expression turned to horror. "Unless you don't want to work at the cafe anymore. Of course not. You own a hotel chain!"

Eve reached over to Juliet and squeezed her hand. "Baking is something I love. You'll have to fire me if you don't want me coming to the cafe."

"Never gonna happen," Juliet confirmed.

"While I plan to stay active in the company, it's not my main focus. It's not my passion."

"Whew!" Juliet wiped a hand across her brow in jest. "I'd miss you if you left."

"I'm here to stay." Eve looked at Griffin, locking her fingers with his. "This is my home."

He'd never tire of hearing that.

"Are you seeing what I'm seeing, Bryce?" Juliet whispered.

Griffin could only chuckle at his sister's bemused face. "Eve's moving in. As soon as I can buy a ring, it will be official that we're getting married as well."

"Oh no, sir. It's official right now, ring or no ring. You asked me to marry you, and I accepted," Eve insisted.

Before Griffin could respond, Juliet was squealing in delight. Congratulations went around the room and the need to argue about it was over and forgotten. Though he'd be buying a ring tomorrow at the latest. He wanted a ring on her finger.

Maybe she'd be up for a Christmas wedding, around the actual holiday.

EPILOGUE

EVE SHIVERED from the cold that followed her inside, then stomped her boots on the rug. The merry tune coming from the speakers made her smile. To think she hated the dratted music when she first arrived. Now she felt lost without hearing it all the time.

She greeted the few customers already in the cafe, chatting as she walked to the kitchen. Chip was deep into kneading the dough at the counter, hopping and bopping to the music.

"Morning, Eve. Looking cold."

She giggled at the assessment because it was true. She'd grown up in Florida all her life, and while she'd traveled around the world at different times, she didn't remember waking up to such coldness before. Minnesota's winter was about to be a rude awakening for her. It started snowing last night and she woke up to at least six inches. It had yet to stop. Griffin had driven her to work, which had eased her worries about driving in the snow. Something she had never done before.

"Why didn't anyone warn me how cold it could get?"

Chip laughed. "You haven't seen anything yet!"

That's what worried her.

"You know, I've gotten used to Christmas during the months you're not supposed to celebrate it, but it's weird how snow adds an extra merriment I didn't realize this town was missing."

"Yeah, fake snow doesn't cut it in the summer months. Real snow is nice." Chip's brows cocked high. "Only for a few weeks though. Give it time and you'll be sick of it real quick. Trust me."

Somehow, she knew she should. Well, she'd enjoy it right now. The whiteness everywhere. The plows making tiny hills in spots. The kids with their smiles. The snowflakes as they filtered to the ground looking so pretty.

"Where's Juliet?" Eve asked as she tossed on her apron. Tabitha had been in the front along with the recently hired girl, Dawn, but Eve had yet to eye Juliet anywhere.

"Running late. Her tires suck, and she's knows it. She got stuck in her driveway."

Twenty minutes later, Juliet arrived via the back. Eve saw Duke's patrol car drive away before the door fully closed. They'd been spending more time together recently, not that Juliet would admit to feelings for the man. Eve had tried to pry, and Juliet had brushed it off.

"Welcome to your first snowfall. What do you think?" Juliet asked as she shook off all the snow from her hat and jacket.

"I love it."

Juliet and Chip made eye contact, rolling their eyes, before laughing together. Eve couldn't help but join in. She knew she'd be hating the snow along with them soon enough.

The day went great as it usually did. In the past few months, she'd gotten into a routine that fit her perfectly. Working at the cafe where she chatted with everyone, getting into the gossip like the rest of them. Going home to Griffin where they were in sync with everything. Cooking supper, maintaining the chores together. Making love.

Griffin had teased her a Christmas wedding would be fun. She declined and insisted at least one thing in her life had to be non-christmasy. In October, along with Juliet and Bryce, they got married in the Bahamas on the beach with the sun setting and the waves crashing. It had been a beautiful day. The breeze lovely. The weather perfect. The people by her side who made her feel like she truly had a family.

By the time evening rolled around, the snow still hadn't let up. Juliet closed the cafe an hour early because the roads hadn't been great all day, and not many people ventured in anyway. Griffin picked her up, his cheeks a rosy red.

"You look tired." She brushed his cheek before kissing him.

"Snow days are never fun. I've responded to more traffic accidents than I care to admit."

Which would explain the rosiness on his face.

"You're going back to work as soon as you drop me off, aren't you?"

He grinned. "Only for a few more hours. I have almost every available officer on duty today because of the weather. You'd think people would be smarter to stay home in weather like this."

"Well, I'll make some soup so you can warm up faster when you get home."

The kiss he delivered said he loved that plan.

The drive home took much longer than the drive into town this morning. She worried when he pulled out of the driveway and left. Pushing the concerns aside, knowing it wouldn't help anyway, she started to cook chicken wild rice soup.

Halfway through, she paused, staring out the window. Her cottage—as she couldn't think of it as anything else— looked serene and picturesque. Snow piled high on the roof, icicles dangling from the gutters. All it needed was smoke coming from a chimney it didn't possess and lights sparkling through the windows.

An idea formed as she stared at it.

When Griffin arrived home a few hours later, she couldn't wait to tell him her idea.

"What do you think about adding the cottage to the hotel?"

His brows puckered, his eyes filled with confusion. "In what way?"

"Well, not just your cottage. But we build other little ones like yours around town. Near the woods, on the outskirts of town to get that picturesque feeling I get while looking outside here. A home away from home. A Christmas vacation getaway like no one has ever experienced. You know the board has been pressuring me to build a hotel around here. They think it would do well in the area. They've been wanting to expand outside of Florida for a while. I've been resistant. You know I have."

He nodded, his eyes lighting with understanding as she continued.

"I don't want a big, stuffy hotel here. This town isn't made for that. It wouldn't fit. But cottages. Personal service. Goodies stocked from the cafe. Christmas at your doorstep. Now that I can see. How hard do you think it would be to add a fireplace and chimney to your cottage? It needs one, don't you think?"

Griffin chuckled as he followed her gaze to look outside. "If you think so, then so do I. You never fail to amaze me."

She snuggled into his embrace as he pulled her closer. "So you're not opposed to the idea?"

"My cottage is your cottage. I think it's a great idea. I also agree, a hotel wouldn't fit here." He cupped her cheeks, kissing her deeply. "But you fit here. You have from the moment you arrived."

"I hated Christmas when I first got here, but if you say so."

He chuckled. "I love you."

"I love you more."

"Oh, no. I love you more more." He grabbed her hand as he guided them out of the kitchen. "I love you so much that I know you want to start planning right this second."

He had her sit down, then grabbed the notepad she always kept on the shelf in the living room and gave it to her along with a pencil. "I can't wait to see all your ideas come to life."

"Like Frosty. It's going to be as magical as that snowman."

"I have no doubt." Griffin kissed her before letting her run wild with ideas.

FOR THE NEXT BOOK IN THIS EXCITING SERIES, CHECK OUT
HERE COMES CHAOS!

Welcome to Sleighville...where mayhem meets murder.

Mayor Bryce Stuart's quaint Christmas town is in crisis. With holiday cheer fading faster than melting snow, he turns to a PR firm for a total holiday makeover. Amidst the tinsel-draped chaos and unexpected divorce papers, Bryce is determined to save his town even as his personal life unravels.

Lila Hansley, a PR whiz, would rather dodge snowflakes than deck the halls. When her grinch of a boss tasks her with reviving a town where yuletide seems cursed, she finds herself tangled in more than just stubborn locals and tacky decorations. Between Bryce's infectious Christmas spirit and his soon-to-be ex-wife's icy interference, Lila's job becomes a real-life holiday mayhem.

But when mischief escalates to murder, Sleighville's revival takes a sinister turn. As tensions rise and secrets surface, Bryce and Lila must navigate a web of small-town intrigue where someone's silent night just became permanent.

Can they uncover the mystery before their Christmas miracle becomes another holiday homicide? Or will Sleighville's dark secrets bury their efforts deeper than the winter snow?

For Duke & Noel's story, check out
The Last Noel
A Sleighville Novel, #3

Welcome to Sleighville...where truth and lies lurk below the surface.

Officer Duke Fisk's life has been one disappointment after another. A cold murder case, married friends while he's the last man standing, and the woman he loves sees him as a brother. When mysterious Noel Lancaster strolls into town giving him sultry looks, he decides it's time for a bit of fun. Just a fling to escape his funk. Except Duke's not built for casual.

Noel Lancaster came to Sleighville for one reason: to find whoever killed her sister. Infiltrating this cheerful town won't be easy when she can't reveal why she's really there. It becomes impossible when she gets involved with Duke—the lead officer on her sister's case.

As Noel digs deeper, dangerous secrets surface along with deadly threats. She knows once Duke learns the truth, he'll hate her forever. But she'll risk everything—her heart and her life—to catch her sister's killer.

Dive into this thrilling holiday romance with a deadly twist, where you'll find merriment and murder all wrapped up with a heart-pounding ending that will leave you breathless.

FOR A SMALL TOWN ROMANTIC SUSPENSE, CHECK OUT...
ESCAPING MEMORIES
A LUCKY TOWN NOVEL, #1

Her past is a deadly puzzle she must solve...before it's too late.

Stumbling into a stranger's isolated cabin, she's terrified—her memories a dangerous blank slate. The only thing her instincts scream is to trust the ruggedly handsome Sheriff Logan Caldwell who found her. With his protective nature and gentle touch, he also makes her feel safer than she has in...well, as long as she can remember.

As shadows of her forgotten past close in, Logan becomes her only ally against an unknown enemy. Every recovered memory brings more fear than answers. As passion ignites between them, one thing becomes clear: if her enemy finds her, she'll meet a fate worse than death.

*With nail-biting suspense and smoldering romance, plunge into the danger and desire with the first book in the **Lucky Town series** today!*

ABOUT THE AUTHOR

I'm a *USA Today* Bestselling Author that loves to write contemporary romance and romantic suspense novels, although I am partial to romantic suspense. I even dabble in paranormal. Honestly, I love anything that has to do with romance. As long as there's a happy ending, I'm a happy camper. And insta-love...yes, please! I love baseball (Go Twins!) and creating awesome crafts. I graduated with a Bachelor's Degree in Criminal Justice, working in that field for several years before I became a stay-at-home mom. I have a few more amazing stories in the works. If you would like to learn more about me and my books, head to my website by scanning the QR code. Thanks for reading!

Scan me